Zane looked up at her. All the protective layers she'd erected that day teetered under the blue intensity of his gaze.

After a long second, he crossed the short distance to her side in one step. He sat on the edge of her mattress.

For several seconds they stared at each other. Kinsey felt as though she was going to explode.

"You look beautiful tonight," he said as he ran a lock of her hair through his fingers. "Of course, you always look beautiful."

"For all the good it does us," she whispered. When he leaned over her and kissed her cheek, she turned her face. "Don't."

"Sorry," he said, and slowly sat up. He didn't leave, however, just sat there, still and silent, one hand on her shoulder as he stared into the room. Finally he looked down at her again.

"Last night I asked you to give me one more day. That day is now over. I think you should drive away tomorrow and let me finish this."

COWBOY INCOGNITO

ALICE SHARPE

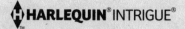

This book is dedicated to the newest member of our family, Tyler Lawrence Shumate. Live long and prosper, sweetie.

ISBN-13: 978-0-373-74888-4

Cowboy Incognito

Copyright © 2015 by Alice Sharpe

Recycling programs for this product may not exist in your area.

Printed in U.S.A.

Alice Sharpe met her husband-to-be on a cold, foggy beach in Northern California. Their union has survived the rearing of two children, a handful of earthquakes, numerous cats and a few special dogs, the latest of which is a yellow Lab named Annie Rose. Alice and her husband now live in a small rural town in Oregon, where she devotes the majority of her time to pursuing her second love, writing. You can write to her c/o Harlequin Books, 233 Broadway, Suite 1001, New York, NY 10279. An SASE for reply is appreciated.

Books by Alice Sharpe

HARLEQUIN INTRIGUE

Visit the Author Profile page at Harlequin.com for more titles.

CAST OF CHARACTERS

Zane Doe—This tall, good-looking cowboy is in New Orleans on a mission until a calculated shove destroys any memory of who he is or what he was up to. It doesn't take long for him to realize an unknown nemesis will stop at nothing to keep it that way.

Kinsey Frost—She's a talented artist with a penchant for painting people. The cowboy first catches her eye, but proceeds to capture her heart. The problem? Somehow her mother is in the middle of his quest—why?

Frances Frost—Kinsey's prickly, nomadic mom has always been an enigma and a responsibility to Kinsey. Is her new lease on life enough to quiet her demons?

Bill Dodge—Frances's employer, this ailing older man was once a person of note in New Orleans.

James Fenwick—Bill Dodge's lawyer has developed a sudden appreciation of Kinsey's mother. That's good, right?

Chad Dodge—Bill's nephew, the kind who can't wait to claim his inheritance. Nobody likes this guy. What in the world is he up to now?

Ryan Jones—A friend of Kinsey's, he seems to have vanished right around the same time Zane was injured. He was also asking about her mom, just as Zane was doing. Is it possible there's a connection?

Jodie Brown—The new wrangler on the Hastings Ranch has everyone nervous. Is his only interest making traveling money or is that foul temper of his covering a deeper, bleaker agenda?

Chance Hastings—The rogue among the brothers would never admit he's in the middle of a love/hate relationship with Lily, the single mother who works on the ranch.

Lily Kirk—Clever, sexy, determined, secretive—she's all that and more. Is her past about to raise its ugly head and exact a terrible price from the wrong person?

Pike Hastings—The handsome, studious-looking brother with a strong back and a deep heart. He's the kind you can trust with secrets.

Frankie Hastings—The brother with the unsavory friends and a penchant for trouble. His most noticeable attribute for now is that he's not around.

Chapter One

Kinsey Frost loved her adopted home of New Orleans no matter what the weather threw at her. Since moving there a few years ago, various storms had flexed their muscles and she'd kind of enjoyed the drama of it all.

However, on a summer day like this, when the humidity hovered close to a drizzle and no breeze blew off the Mississippi River, mixed feelings tended to sneak their way in. Add a crowded hot sidewalk, time restraint and a sore back from climbing up and down a ladder all day and she was about five seconds away from hailing a cab to take her the six blocks home. She was painfully aware she had an hour to take a shower, change her clothes and return to the gallery she'd just left.

That was cutting it close and she decided on the spot that once she had cleaned herself up, she would drive back to the gallery instead of walking as she usually did.

To take her mind off her wilting condition, she

focused on her fellow pedestrians. As an artist, she was always interested in people watching, even when they had their backs to her. Directly ahead walked a woman who had twisted her hair into an intricate knot and secured it with what looked like red chopsticks. In front of her two businessmen in lightweight suits argued about something, their profiles twisted with emotion. Then came a woman wearing a pink dress who held the hands of two little girls. Twins? Probably, as they were the same size and wore identical clothes.

Looking even farther ahead, Kinsey caught a glimpse of a tan Stetson hat. She tilted her head to see on whom it perched and found a tall guy with dark hair touching the back of his shirt collar. A black leather vest stretched across broad shoulders. Through the legs of those between them, she caught sight of jeans and black boots.

This was not Bourbon Street. Few tourists visited this area at five o'clock on a Friday afternoon, fewer still dressed like this man. She watched him for another half block, struck by his steady gait and the aura he emitted of knowing where he was going and what he was going to do when he got there. She couldn't help being curious about his ultimate destination.

Life was full of interesting people with fascinating stories you never had a chance to know. Right now, for Kinsey, the far more pressing issue was time. The gallery was holding an opening-night show for an "outstanding new talent." That's what the owner called anyone to whom he dedicated wall space and a wine-and-cheese party. In Kinsey's opinion, this time he was dead-on right. She'd spent most of the day hanging one beautiful painting after another, striving to suit both owner and finicky artist. No doubt there would be a fair amount of hand-holding required that evening.

The light on the corner changed and the crowd up ahead slowed down to wait it out. Kinsey had lost track of the cowboy, but now he caught her attention again. He stood at the edge of the sidewalk, slightly apart. The giggling antics of the two little girls apparently caught his attention and he turned. As though he sensed Kinsey's stare, his gaze darted from the children straight to her.

The word *handsome* didn't do him justice, didn't begin to hint at the smoldering warmth of his eyes, the curiosity, the intelligence. His tan was deep, his eyes an unexpected blue, his brows straight and dark. He appeared to be several years her senior, maybe in his midthirties, and she'd bet a bundle he was better looking now than he'd been a decade before. That's what bones like his could do for a man…

Very slowly and with more than a taste of speculation, his sensual lips twitched into a smile as he returned her appraisal. Dazzled and a bit embarrassed to have been caught staring, Kinsey immediately looked away.

And that's how she came to be facing the bicyclist speeding down the middle of the sidewalk, scattering pedestrians like a stiff wind blowing through fallen leaves. She hastily stepped out of the way as he whizzed past, the yellow vest the company's pedaling messengers wore flying out behind him. The matching helmet obscured his features. Kinsey twirled to face the corner and shout a warning, but it seemed everyone had already sensed something amiss. Someone dropped a shopping bag and someone else screamed. The woman with the children grabbed each girl by a hand and dragged them to the shelter of a recessed doorway, but one of them pulled free. Laughing as though caught up in a game, she shot out onto the sidewalk.

The weirdest mixture of slow motion and fast-forward came over Kinsey as she soundlessly watched events unfold. The child suddenly stopped dead in her tracks, struck now by the approaching danger but obviously afraid to move. The cowboy dashed to sweep the girl out of harm's way. The cyclist veered closer to them and then like a flash, unexpected and unreal, he let go of the right grip and shoved the still-moving cowboy, connecting with his shoulder, upsetting his precarious balance. The push propelled man and child toward the street at the same instant a cab cut the corner too close and the cowboy stumbled into its path. The cab stopped abruptly, the driver's face through the windshield one of abject terror.

The screech of brakes and blare of horns masked the collective gasp of the onlookers. The cyclist had gone down, too, but he'd rolled to his feet and now went to the aid of the fallen. As he hovered over them, the momentum created by the flow of traffic speeding by in the other direction caused his yellow vest to whip around his torso like the wings of a wounded butterfly.

The crowd began moving again. Kinsey hesitated just a second, then dashed into the street, heedless now of her aching muscles and sweating brow. As she closed the distance, the cyclist hopped up, ran to his bike, somehow managed to mount it and pedal away down the sidewalk like nobody's business.

The child, still caught in the cowboy's slack embrace, whimpered. The man lay still as death. Kinsey leaned over them as the woman in pink appeared, screaming something in what sounded like Swedish, while the little girl who hadn't been injured sobbed uncontrollably by her side. Kinsey set her fingers against the man's throat and felt the flutter of his heartbeat, saw the flickering of his lashes. The child's eyes were open, but her skin was pale and she looked dazed. Someone touched Kinsey's shoulder.

"I'm a doctor," a middle-aged woman said. "Please, move aside, let me see them." Kinsey stood and backed out of the way, one hand covering her mouth, unaware of the bloodstains on her white jeans.

AMBULANCES SHOWED UP and soon after, the police. The taxi driver had finally emerged, white faced and shaken. One policeman led him away from everyone else for an interview. Kinsey was questioned along with the other onlookers. Of course, officials were very anxious to hear about the cyclist, and Kinsey discovered she was one of only two people who'd actually seen the shove. Attention of the others seemed to have been focused on the child or even the taxi. Kinsey could offer very little description of the aggressor as it had all happened in such a blur and the helmet had hidden his features.

They wanted to know if it looked as if the cowboy and the cyclist knew each other, or if the child had been the target. They wanted to know if she could recall anything that implied malice. As she watched the ambulance crew load the child and man into separate vehicles and drive away, she blinked rapidly. "Nothing," she admitted. "Except the shove, of course."

By luck, someone had been using their phone

to record the twin girls and had caught the incident. Hopefully, the video would reveal things that had happened too fast for the human eye to spot.

"We're going to go to the hospital now to find out more about the victims," one of the officers told Kinsey as he wrote down her name and number in his notebook. "If you think of anything, anything at all, call me."

"What about the company the messenger worked for?" she asked. "Speedy Courier, isn't that the name? Maybe they can identify which of their messengers were on this street today."

"We're checking into that," the officer assured her. He handed her his card and she scanned it quickly. His name was Edward Woods. He nodded at her and walked away toward his car. A second later, Kinsey called out to him.

"Detective Woods? There is something," she said. "Your footsteps just now…" Her voice trailed off as she fought to organize her thoughts. "When the courier ran off, I heard the slap of his shoes."

The detective's shoulders shrugged with uncertainty as to her point.

"I see these messengers all the time," she explained. "My mother lives in one of those beautiful old houses a couple of miles farther up the avenue and the gallery I work at is only two blocks from here. I shop at the little grocery right up the street… Anyway, all the couriers around here dress the same. Their vests are always zipped. This one wasn't. Plus, they all wear black formfitting bike pants and specialty sports shoes, you know?"

Light began to dawn in Woods's eyes. "Sports shoes," he repeated. "With rubber soles."

"Yes. I think this guy was wearing loafers. His feet made a sound just like yours did. He might have been in slacks, too, maybe tucked into dark socks. I can't quite recall."

"You still can't remember anything about his face?"

"No."

The detective sighed.

As she headed home, Kinsey used her cell to arrange backup for the gallery show. The time when she should have returned had come and gone, and once again, a sense of urgency propelled her toward her apartment. The door closing behind her gave a fleeting sense of security and the desire to sit in front of a fan and catch her breath almost overwhelmed her. Instead of giving in to it, she took a hurried shower, pulled on a black dress, pinned up her damp hair and returned to the gallery.

The opening party was in full swing by the time Kinsey found a parking spot and walked through the door. Her boss, Marc Costello, caught her eye and gestured for her to join him.

Together, they moved to a private alcove, greeting guests before bending their heads to speak.

"I heard about what happened out on the street," Marc said. He was about fifty with a shock of silver hair and looked the part of a gallery owner right down to his black turtleneck worn under a stylish black silk jacket. Not exactly summery New Orleans attire, but that wasn't what he was interested in anyway. "Are you all right?"

"I'm fine," she assured him.

"I have to tell you something. Right about the time of that accident, your boyfriend, Ryan Jones, was in here. He was asking a whole lot of questions."

Kinsey instantly conjured an image of Ryan: curly blond hair, bittersweet-chocolate eyes, a nice smile. She'd met him several weeks earlier when he came into the gallery to buy a painting for his office and wound up taking Kinsey to dinner instead. Since then, she saw him whenever his New York engineering firm sent him to New Orleans to work on a levee project they'd contracted. "What kind of questions?" she asked.

"Stuff about your background, where you'd grown up, things like that."

Kinsey's brow wrinkled. "What did you tell him?"

"Nothing. You haven't exactly told me a whole

lot, you know. I just said something about what a hard worker you are. He said he knew that. Then he started asking questions about your family, specifically, your mother."

Kinsey swallowed hard. "My mother? What did he want to know?"

"Let's see. How old she was and how long had she lived here and where exactly did she live and work…stuff like that. I told him the truth, that I'd never met her, that she was kind of a recluse. He left a few minutes later after getting a phone call."

"That's…odd," Kinsey said. She'd spent years looking after her mother who at times was a social misfit. The thought of a friend asking questions behind her back—well, it was disquieting.

"I thought so, too. That's why I'm telling you." He took a deep breath and added, "On top of that, I'm afraid we have a more immediate problem than a snoopy boyfriend."

"Don't keep calling him my boyfriend," she protested. "We haven't known each other that long and he's only in town—"

Marc held up a hand. "Yeah, yeah, yeah, you know what I mean. Our star artist is holed up in the ladies' room."

Still reeling over news that Ryan had been asking about her family, Kinsey shook her head. "How long has she been in there?"

"Forever. Someone from the newspaper showed

up and wanted an interview and she refused. Turned all shy, refused to have her picture taken or anything. Thank goodness you're here. She's supposed to say something meaningful about her muse in five minutes. Remind her that's why I'm doing this show, to sell her work, not be her therapist."

"I know, Marc. I'll get her back out here."

"Tell her the newspaper guy left."

"Did he?"

"Yeah. I tried to get him to stay, but art shows aren't exactly a huge draw, even when the paintings are as good as these."

The opening seemed to be well attended, for which Kinsey was thankful. She'd sent out over a hundred invitations and it looked as if about half had decided to come, packing the narrow, trendy space with well-dressed people sipping wine. Of course, it was a heck of a lot cooler in the gallery than it was outside, so maybe that helped account for some of the attendees.

As she moved through the room, greeting people as she went, she noticed several discreet sold signs. That should make Marc happy.

Once inside the ladies "lounge," Kinsey found Ellen Rhodes sitting forlornly on a velvet bench, staring at her hands.

"Congratulations, you're a hit," Kinsey said with a giant smile.

Ellen looked up with nervous blue eyes. "I

can't do this. I don't like all these people looking at my work."

"Isn't that the point of a show?" Kinsey asked gently.

"I didn't know it would be like this. So many people…"

"You've already sold several paintings," Kinsey said. "You're a hit."

"I just want to go home."

"Listen, I get it, you're not into the publicity side of things, you're not a media hound. But Marc has a lot at stake here. He believes in your work or he wouldn't have offered you this show. Most artists work for recognition, you know. Buck up, now."

"You sound like my mother," Ellen said, but at least there was a little snap in her voice.

"That's because I'm channeling my own," Kinsey said. "I've heard versions of this speech my whole life." Like when she'd come home from a school she'd only attended a month to find her mother packing…again. No matter how much Kinsey pleaded to stay in one place, they inevitably moved on. When Mom got it in her head it was time to go, they went. Period.

Until a few years ago, that is. As soon as Kinsey had announced her independence and settled down in New Orleans, her mother had followed suit. She now took care of a sickly elderly man who had once been wealthy but was no longer, and she seemed almost content.

"Is that newspaper guy still out there?"

"No. Marc gave him an interview and he left." Kinsey's cell phone rang and she slipped it out of her pocket, answering hesitantly when she didn't recognize the number. She listened for a minute or so before responding in a soft voice.

"Is everything okay?" Ellen asked as Kinsey pushed the end-call button.

Kinsey dropped her phone into her evening bag. "Huh? Oh, yes. And no." She made a decision and added, "I'm really sorry, but I have to leave."

"You can't," Ellen squealed.

"I have to. That was the police."

"The police!"

"They want my help with an accident victim. I have to go to the hospital right away."

Ellen started to protest, but Kinsey hustled her back into the main gallery and steered her toward Marc, who couldn't hide the look of relief that flooded his face.

"Are you feeling better?" he asked Ellen.

"I was until Kinsey said she's leaving."

Marc's smile drooped as he turned his attention to Kinsey. "You can't leave. You just got here."

"I'm sorry, but the man who was hit earlier

this evening is conscious and the police asked me to come see him."

"Why you?"

"They didn't say."

"But you don't even know him!"

"I know," Kinsey agreed. "I'll be back as soon as I can," she called as she raced outside, car keys in hand.

A half hour later, she stepped out of the elevator onto the third floor of the hospital. She immediately spotted Detective Woods standing at the end of a short corridor as though waiting for her.

"I can see I took you away from something special," he said with an appraising glance at her dress. He himself wore the same light blue sports jacket he'd worn earlier.

"I was at a work-related event," she explained.

"Well, it was good of you to take time out for this. We appreciate it."

"I don't know what I can possibly do to help," she said. "Is he in this room?"

The detective glanced at the door in front of them. "Yes, but I'd like to speak to you for a moment before we go in. Can I get you a cup of coffee or a glass of ice water?"

"No, thanks."

The hospital had placed two chairs by the window at the end of the corridor and he gestured for her to sit. "First of all," he began as they settled into the chairs, "you were right. The cyclist you and the others saw wasn't a messenger for Speedy Courier. The real one claims he'd just finished a delivery and was stooping to unlock his bike when someone bashed him over the head. He'd left his helmet looped over the handlebars while he made the delivery. Anyway, when he came to, he found his bike, helmet and vest were missing. He has no idea who did it. He showed up back at the Speedy office to report it about the same time we showed up asking questions."

"So the guy we saw was a phony," Kinsey said.

"Yep. We're retracing the real messenger's trail to see if anyone he made deliveries to noticed anything peculiar. By the way, he's a very thin, small young man. I imagine the thief couldn't get the zipper up on the vest and that's why it was open. Oh, and the phone video showed just what you surmised. The guy was wearing slacks and loafers."

"The real messenger is okay?"

"He's got a bump, but he's fine."

"And how about the little girl the cowboy saved? Is she all right?"

"Released an hour or so ago. The woman with her and her sister was the new au pair. I think she was more traumatized than the kids. By cowboy, are you referring to our John Doe?"

"That's how I thought of him," she said, nodding toward the room. "Because of the hat and everything. Wait a second, John Doe? You don't know who he is?"

"No."

"But his wallet—"

"Is missing. We think the cyclist must have taken it. And before you ask, no cell phone, just a key chain with six keys on it."

Was that what the cyclist had been doing while everyone thought he was trying to help? Stealing the cowboy's identity? It had to be. She racked her brain for an image of him pocketing something and came up blank, but he'd had his back to her and that bright vest flapping around him. "Did the taxi driver see anything?" she asked.

"He claims just about everyone on the ground was out of his line of sight. I had someone check that out and he's telling the truth, they were too close to the front of the cab for the driver to see what was going on."

"Wait a second," Kinsey said as she finally made sense of what the detective had said a couple of sentences earlier. "You said the cowboy is conscious. Can't he just tell you his name?"

The detective shook his head. "He doesn't remember who he is. In fact, he doesn't remember anything. And we have no way of knowing if this condition is recent or ongoing because no one has come forward to ask for a missing man, let alone one fitting his description."

Kinsey sat back on the chair a second. "If this amnesia just started because of the incident today, is there a chance it could go away by morning?"

"The doctors say it's anyone's guess. He could start remembering his identity in five minutes, five days or five years. Apparently lots of people with head injuries forget segments of their lives, usually just the few minutes preceding their accident. Anyway, chances are good someone who does know him will show up sooner rather than later. For now, we only have one lead."

"And what's that?" Kinsey asked.

"You."

Kinsey perked up immediately. "Me? What are you talking about?"

"Your name was written on a piece of paper we found in his pocket. Can you think of a reason for that?"

"None," she said.

"And you're sure you've never seen him before?"

"Pretty sure," Kinsey said. "I guess it's possible I ran into him sometime in the past. I've lived in a fair number of cities all across the country." Even as she spoke, she found herself doubting it could be true. John Doe, for lack of a real name, was an arresting-looking man. Would she have forgotten someone who appealed to her on such a gut level?

Woods sighed as he got to his feet. "Would you come with me to meet the guy? Maybe it will jar a memory if you hear his voice."

"Of course," Kinsey said, ignoring the pounding of her heart. She had no idea why she felt so nervous. Sweaty palms defied the hospital's efficient air-conditioning system.

Suppressing a shiver, she followed Woods into the room.

Chapter Two

Despite his throbbing head, he fell into a black-and-white world of disjointed collages. It was a relief when a noise shook him out of the nothingness of his dreamworld. Even as he gingerly rubbed his eyes, he recognized the sound the door made when it opened and closed.

He looked up, expecting to see the cop who had asked him questions earlier or one of the doctors or nurses who were taking care of him. He did not expect to find himself staring into the velvety-brown eyes of a small woman wearing a formfitting black dress that revealed creamy smooth shoulders and a modest hint of cleavage.

He lifted his gaze back to the oval perfection of her face and hoped that he and she were long-time lovers, that she would run to him, throw her arms around him and whisper his name in his ear before planting her succulent red lips right on his. He wanted a name. He wanted an identity. He wanted his past, and maybe she was the key. If so, she made a heck of a sexy key and he was prepared to earn his memory back one succulent kiss at a time.

Her response to his gaze was a nervous twitch of her lips. He tried a reassuring smile, but that stretched the three stitches in his left cheek and he grimaced.

The woman did not look as though she loved him. Hell, she didn't even look as though she knew him.

"You must be Kinsey Frost," he said.

Now she just looked spooked. Her eyes grew wide. "Do you know me?"

"I don't even know me," he admitted. He nodded toward the cop standing behind her. "Detective Woods told me they found the name Kinsey Frost on a piece of paper. I just assumed you're her."

Some of the uneasiness fled from her face. "Oh, I see."

"I'm hoping you have answers for me," he added.

She shook her head. "I'm sorry. Today is the first time I ever saw you. I'm sure of it." She narrowed her eyes as she looked him over and nodded. "You were walking ahead of me down the sidewalk and you caught my attention because of your hat. But I don't know you."

His hand flew to his head. "I was wearing a hat?" He directed his gaze to Woods. "Where is it?"

"It fell off when you tumbled into the street. A car going the other way nailed it."

"What kind of hat?" he asked.

Kinsey supplied the answer. "A tan Stetson. It looked kind of new and very nice."

He glanced down at his hands. He'd already noticed calluses and deeply tanned skin, along with old scars, on his knuckles. "Workingman hands," he said softly. Not the hands of a teacher or a doctor. The hands of a man who got down and dirty on occasion, and instinctively, he knew at least that much about himself. He looked up at Woods. "And I was wearing cowboy boots. That's what the nurse said."

"That's right," Detective Woods concurred. "Plus, you don't sound like you're from around here. In fact, you don't have much of an accent at all. We're checking hotels to see if any of their customers are unaccounted for, but it's questionable anything will come of it. There are thousands of rooms in this city. It's unlikely anyone has missed you yet, unless you didn't show up for an appointment or something. The big question is why you were carrying Ms. Frost's name. What's the link between you two?"

"I hope that's a rhetorical question and you aren't expecting an answer from me," he said. He looked at Kinsey again. "It's up to you."

Her hand brushed his arm. "I'm sorry," she

said. "I can't imagine why you were carrying my name."

"In addition to working at the gallery, you're also an artist yourself, aren't you?" Woods asked.

She turned to look at him. "Yes."

"Could he have gotten your name from a third party in relation to your work?"

"I guess so. I've done several portraits for people in New Orleans since I moved here a couple of years ago." She glanced back at him with a question in her eyes. "Maybe one of them gave you my name and you were trying to find the gallery to talk to me."

"He was walking away from, not headed to, the gallery," the detective pointed out with a frown.

"People sometimes have a hard time finding the place. It's very narrow. Maybe he walked right past it."

"We'll question people on that street as time and manpower allow," the detective said. "Including Marc Costello. But as you know, it's a long one with several businesses and homes farther along…it's going to take a while. I'd appreciate it if you would also make a list of the people you did work for so we can ask them if they might have given your name to the…victim." The detective shook his head as he looked at the bed. "Sorry, I'm not sure what to call you."

"Don't worry about it," he said.

The detective scanned his notebook briefly before directing a comment to Kinsey. "When I questioned you right after the incident, you said he was walking with determination, that he appeared preoccupied."

Kinsey nodded thoughtfully.

"That doesn't sound like he was searching for something to me."

"I guess it doesn't," Kinsey agreed.

The detective opened a small manila envelope he pulled from a jacket pocket and shook out a set of keys.

"Those are the keys you showed me earlier," he said. "The ones they found in my pocket."

"Yes," Woods said. "I wanted you to hold them, look at them, see if they jog a memory." He pointed at the fob, a small disk decorated with a red tractor and the words *Red Hot, St. George, Utah*. "We checked on that, by the way."

"It sounds like a strip club," he said.

The detective laughed. "Yeah, that's what we thought, too. What it really is, though, is a nickname for a small tractor. We found the dealership that carries it, name of Travers's Tractors. They're not missing anyone, but we did fax the police there your photo. They showed it to the staff at the dealership…didn't get any hits, but a couple of people are on vacation, so they'll try again in a few days. They also have a couple of other stores in their chain and they said they'd ask around and get back to me, but we're also contacting them. Keep in mind that sooner or later someone will wonder what happened to you and report it to the police." His phone rang and he stepped away from the bed to answer it.

Kinsey gestured at all the machines. "Are your other injuries serious?"

"Not as bad as they could have been," he replied, glancing at each key in turn.

"Were you out long?"

"I woke up in the ambulance."

"And you didn't know who you were? That must have been terrifying."

He ran his fingers over the tractor logo and shook his head before meeting her velvety gaze again. "It wasn't like that. What I was aware of was that I didn't know where I was or what had happened to me. There was an oxygen mask over my mouth and nose and my head hurt. I felt confused. I guess there are just certain instances when you decide to wait it out and see what happens. I mean, I could hear the siren, there was a guy sitting next to me who smiled and I was obviously being cared for. That was enough. At first."

"So you have a concussion?"

"And apparently a hard head, too. There's bruising and scrapes, a few stitches, stuff like that, but no broken bones, just this fog where my brain used to be. Thank goodness the taxi didn't hit me or the child I had in my arms."

"The child you saved," Kinsey said.

He smiled, ignoring the stress on the stitches. He liked the way her voice softened as she spoke, the look in her eyes as she met his gaze. "Anyway, the doctors said I was lucky." He paused for a second. Truth was, he didn't feel real lucky right that moment. He'd gladly exchange a broken arm for the return of his memory. "Thanks for trying to help," he added. His gaze followed a few strands of dark hair that had pulled loose from the pins atop her head and trailed down along her cheeks, brushing her collarbone, framing her face. She looked as if she'd stepped out of a dream, and he had another gut feeling about himself. He was a sucker for brunettes with red lips. "You were at a party or something, right?"

Her smile lit up her eyes. "The dress gave it away, huh?"

"More or less."

"We were hosting an opening show for a local artist at the gallery," she said. After a slight pause, she added, "I wish I knew what to call you. John Doe seems kind of impersonal."

"You're artistic," he said. "Give me a name, something that you think fits."

She narrowed her eyes as she studied his features. Then she smiled. "My father died before I was born, but my mother told me that he read constantly and what he liked best were Westerns. She said his favorite author was a guy named Zane Grey. How about we call you Zane?"

"Zane," he murmured. "I like it. Okay, thanks."

She nodded as the detective returned. It was obvious he'd overheard some of their conversation when he raised his eyebrows and said, "Zane?"

"My new alias."

"It fits you," the detective said. "Well, Zane, we've found the bike the fake courier used abandoned in a hallway of an old building due for demolition. I'm going to go check it out. The doctors want to keep you here for several days."

"Who's going to pay for that?" he asked.

"Don't worry about it."

"I don't think I can handle being cooped up in this place for long," Zane admitted. "I think I may be an outdoor type of guy."

Woods narrowed his eyes. "Try to remember that someone took a huge risk today to steal your wallet and probably a cell phone. He pushed you into traffic in front of a crowd of onlookers. It could have just as easily wound up with him in the street as it did you and the child. That underscores this person's recklessness."

"I wonder what was worth such a risk," Zane mused.

"We may never know."

"Did the video help you identify the man who attacked Zane?" Kinsey asked.

The detective shook his head. "He never turned around and looked at anyone." He glanced at Zane again. "Listen, you're safe here. And if you remember anything at all, call me. I left my card on the table by your phone."

Zane had been holding the keys, turning them over and over in his fingers. The detective nodded at them. "Are they bringing back any memories?"

"No," Zane admitted. "Afraid not." He started to hand them back, but the detective held up a hand. "No, that's okay. We made copies, you hold on to those. The doctor said something familiar might jog your memory, and those keys are about all we can offer. That and what's left of your clothes in the cabinet over there."

"The keys are easier to hold," Zane said.

"Exactly." Woods nodded his goodbye to Kinsey and hurried from the room.

Kinsey took a deep breath. "I guess I'd better go, too. It was nice to meet you, Zane."

"Do you have to leave?" he asked. Then he smiled. "Of course you do. You have to get back to work."

"I could stay for a few minutes," she told him.

A panicky knot in his gut followed a moment of pleasure. What in the world did they have to say to each other? He couldn't talk about himself, he couldn't talk about places he'd visited or things he'd seen because he didn't know, he wasn't sure.

She leaned one hip against the bed and looked at him expectantly.

"So, you noticed me because of my hat," he said when no other topic sprang to mind.

That's right," she said.

"But we didn't exchange a word?"

"Not one."

"Did I notice you?"

She looked almost embarrassed. "Kind of. I mean, our eyes did meet one time and you smiled at me."

"I bet I did," he said.

"And then everything started to happen."

"Yeah, the detective told me. Listen, be honest," he added, straightening up and trying to appear dignified. He was finding out that hospital beds weren't designed to make a man look virile and strong, and for some reason, that's how he wanted to look for her. "Did I appear to be a cowboy, you know, a real wrangler type, or did I look like someone who wanted to be a cowboy?"

"You mean, did you look like the real deal or a poser?"

"Exactly," he said, nodding.

She thought for a second. Even doing nothing but thinking looked good on her and it gave him a chance to admire the sweet curve of her lips and the shape of her earlobe.

"Well?" he prompted.

"This is just an impression, you understand. Your clothes looked expensive and new, but you wore them like you'd been born in them. To me, you looked like a guy who was on a mission."

He thought about that for a minute. "Do I look like the kind of guy who asks you to paint his portrait?"

"Not really, though everyone is different. Anyway, maybe it's not your own portrait you wanted painted. Maybe it was someone in your family. Your wife or your kids."

He held up his left hand. "No ring, no white line where one has been."

"Lots of hardworking guys don't wear rings," she told him. "Maybe you work with big equipment, like at a mill or something. And if you have a wife, she must be wondering where you are."

"One would hope," he said, and they stared at each other for a few seconds, the silence broken when the door opened and a petite blonde nurse bustled into the room.

"Time for our meds," she chirped.

Kinsey straightened up. "I'd better go," she said.

Zane heard a note of relief in her voice. How

could he blame her? He caught her hand and squeezed it. "Thanks again, Kinsey."

She stared at their linked hands for a second before raising her gaze to his face. "When your memory returns, let me know, okay?" She took a pen from her purse and scrawled her phone number on the back of the detective's card.

"If you're in this neck of the woods tomorrow, drop in and say hi," he told her as she handed him the card. "For all intents and purposes, you're the only friend I have." He winced and shook his head. "Did that sound pathetic enough?"

"You're going to be fine," she told him, her dark eyes soft, her voice barely a whisper.

The nurse handed Zane a small paper sleeve with a pill nestled inside. She picked up his water glass, shook it until the ice inside rattled. "I'll go get you more water. Back in a sec." As the door closed behind her, Kinsey spared Zane one last smile and then she was gone, too.

He laid his head back against the pillow and studied the pill. He hoped this was the one that would help him sleep and he welcomed the prospect. Maybe tomorrow he'd wake up a new man…or rather the man he used to be.

But before he took that pill, he was determined to get on his feet and walk. Something inside urged him to remain strong and vigilant. He hoped the nurse didn't give him any flak.

As KINSEY WALKED to the parking garage, she dug her cell phone from her purse. She'd silenced it when she arrived at the hospital and now she turned the sound back on.

As expected, there were several calls from Marc. Not expected were the three from her mother. Marc's messages were all the same: come back to the gallery! Her mother left no messages. And there wasn't one from Ryan, either, who always called when he got into town. The absence of that call coupled with his earlier questions made Kinsey nervous, but why? There was probably a harmless explanation, and she intended on finding out what it was. She called Ryan's cell number and left a message when the phone switched immediately to voice mail.

By now the show at the gallery was over. The crew engaged to clean up after the gala would be hard at work. Kinsey called her boss, half wondering if he'd fire her on the spot.

"It all turned out okay," Marc said. In the background, Kinsey heard voices and the tinkling of glass. It sounded as if Marc had gone out to eat after the show. "We sold eight of her paintings. Everyone loved her once she lightened up."

"I'm sorry I had to leave," Kinsey said as she unlocked her car door.

"Couldn't be helped," Marc said. His voice was muffled, as though he had covered the phone to speak to someone else, and she waited a second or two before he got back to her. "Listen, it's time to order and I'm starving. I'll see you tomorrow."

Food. When had she last eaten, lunchtime? Her stomach growled.

She contemplated calling her mother and decided against it. There was one phone in the old house. Her mother was and always had been something of a night owl, but the man she took care of would be asleep by now and Kinsey didn't want to wake him.

Those three calls were worrisome, though. Had Ryan somehow found out where she lived and, heaven forbid, had he visited her?

That would not do. If there was one thing Kinsey knew, it was her mom didn't like strangers. Frances Frost was obligated now to Mr. Dodge, but the poor old guy couldn't live forever. Sooner or later, she'd be free to wander off again and perhaps if pushed, would do so sooner rather than later.

Three calls meant something had gotten to her. Kinsey knew she'd never be able to sleep if she didn't see her mom in the flesh and make sure everything was okay. At the last second, she stopped at the small grocery located about midway between the Dodge house and the art gallery to pick up something—anything—to eat. She was met at the door by the Chinese owner,

Henry Lee, who was getting ready to turn the open sign to closed.

"Can I grab something really quick?" she asked. "I'm famished."

"Sure," he said, allowing her to enter though turning the sign to discourage further patrons.

Kinsey grabbed a premade po'boy sandwich and a bottle of iced tea. A basket on the counter held bananas and apples and she added one of each.

"I heard the show was a good one," Mr. Lee said as he totaled her purchases.

"I didn't get to attend much of it," Kinsey admitted as she handed over a twenty-dollar bill. "You heard about the accident down the street?"

"I heard one of those courier guys went berserk and drove into a crowd of people," Mr. Lee said as he counted out Kinsey's change. "I can't tell you how many times one has come close to clipping me."

Kinsey gave Mr. Lee an abbreviated rundown of what had really happened, causing the man's faint eyebrows to arch in surprise. But then his forehead wrinkled. "Did you say the victim wore a cowboy hat?"

"Yes, a tan Stetson. Why?"

Mr. Lee swore under his breath. "I knew there was something I wanted to tell you. A man was in the store earlier today. A cowboy. I swear, he stood right where you are asking questions about someone named Smith. Mary Smith. I think that was the name. Maybe it was Sherry. Anyway, I told him I didn't know anyone by that name. Then he asked about Mr. Dodge's housekeeper."

"By name?"

"No. He called her a housekeeper."

"What did you tell him?" Kinsey asked, trying to remain unflappable. She wasn't sure Henry Lee knew she was even related to the Dodge housekeeper.

"I didn't tell him anything. You have to understand that back in the day, Bill Dodge used his money to do a lot of good in this neighborhood for people like me. You'd have a hard time meeting a kinder man, and I wouldn't send trouble his way for anything. He deserves to live out his life in peace, and as far as I'm concerned, that housekeeper of his allows that to happen. Without her to shoo people away, that worthless nephew of his would walk off with half the house. Anyway, the cowboy guy asked a couple of questions. He was holding up the line in back of him and people were getting restless. He asked about other contacts he could talk to. I recalled seeing you and the housekeeper chatting with each other one day—it's the only time I ever saw that woman talk to anyone in here— so I wrote your name on a piece of paper and said you might know something. Frankly, I was trying to get rid of him. He got busy on his cell phone, I suppose looking you up, then he left. That's it."

"Did you indicate my connection to the gallery?"

"No. I just gave him your name and told him to phone you. You have to understand, it was really crowded in here. I didn't have time to be answering questions, especially when the Gastner sisters started arguing about which one of them got the last box of beignet mix. Half my customers walked out. I completely forgot about the man until right now."

"Did he mention any facts about himself? You know, like where he was from or his name, anything at all?"

"No. I don't think so. I was kind of distracted."

"You need to tell the police about this," Kinsey said. "Ask to speak to Detective Woods."

"I will."

"It could be important," she added. At least she wouldn't have to make a list of her former clients now that this issue would be cleared up. "But maybe you could leave Mr. Dodge and his housekeeper out of it."

"Gotcha," he said with a nod. "I was going to do that anyway because I don't want to trouble Bill."

She left a few minutes later, her head swimming with all that had happened today and what it could possibly mean. Back in her car, she unwrapped the po'boy and took a bite. Was it possible Zane and Ryan were somehow connected, or was it coincidence that two men had asked questions about her mom on the same day and that one wasn't responding to her calls and the other had come close to being killed?

Surely Ryan would realize Marc would report his questions to Kinsey. She was tempted to think it was out of character for Ryan to go behind her back, but truth be known, she wasn't sure exactly what kind of character he had. He'd come on pretty strong, but now that she really thought of it, he hadn't shared much about himself. She knew he was working on a levee project, but she didn't know which one.

Seamlessly, she shifted gears to think about the man she'd given the name Zane, but for a second, she couldn't get past his blue eyes. Paul Newman eyes, with the same frank evaluation going on behind them. It was pretty obvious now that he hadn't wanted Kinsey to paint his portrait because he hadn't asked Mr. Lee directly about her.

On the other hand, she knew just how she'd like to capture him if she did have the opportunity. The sexy twinkle of his eyes, the slight cleft in his chin, his cheekbones and lips. She'd pose him straight on, his rock-hard torso and broad shoulders encased in a trim T-shirt to reveal his muscular arms, head slightly bent forward, thinking about horses or tractors or engines or whatever it was a guy like him thought about when he contemplated life.

Like his wife? Like his girlfriend of thirteen years? How about his six kids?

Hey, this was a fantasy. She could give him any life she wanted because it was doubtful she'd ever see him again.

In fairness to both of them, he'd also exhibited traces of humor that appealed to her, and she hadn't missed the speculative nature of his perusal of her. She knew he was brave and selfless because of the lightning-fast way he'd stepped in to save the little girl, and she knew he was resilient because of how quickly he was attempting to put this behind him and move on. How horrible it must be for a man of action to be frozen in one place and in one moment. It must be like walking out of a warm, cozy room into a blizzard and having the door slam and lock behind you.

Bill Dodge's house was an old Victorian painted a ghastly purple that Kinsey imagined had actually improved as the sun faded the color and the trees matured and concealed the full impact of all that paint. The roofs were steep and Kinsey knew the top floor and attic were seldom used anymore. At eighty years and ailing, Mr. Dodge was too feeble to climb the stairs and slept in a downstairs room that had once been his den. Her mother slept in the housekeeper's room located behind the kitchen. The arrangement seemed to work for both of them.

Kinsey climbed the stairs onto what had once been a beautiful wraparound deck, screened in for summer sleeping when the house was too hot. The screens were torn now and the deck was wobbly. The neighborhood was still good, and while this house had probably once upon a time been a showpiece, now it was like the poor, shabby relation. In some ways, the house reminded Kinsey of an elegant woman who slept on a park bench—still lovely, but rumpled, worn, tired.

At least there was a slight breeze blowing now, making the air bearable. Kinsey wished she'd gone home first to change out of her cocktail dress into shorts because she'd known the downstairs of this house could get stifling. Hopefully, she'd be out of here and on her way home in a few minutes. The day seemed to have lasted a week and she was tired.

Before she announced her presence, she took a deep breath. Dealing with her mom was never easy, and doing so when something had prompted her to call three times suggested trouble.

As Kinsey raised her hand to knock, the door flew open.

Chapter Three

Zane. The name was growing on him, settling into the creases of his very empty brain.

Kinsey Frost's face flashed in his mind and he suspected there was a silly grin on his face as he reconstructed her. She was so darn pretty. There was something else about her, too, something kind of sweet and innocent. Or maybe his response had more to do with the fact hers was the only face he could conjure that wasn't related to people employed to take care of him. She'd come to help out of kindness and perhaps curiosity, which was totally understandable, considering they were strangers.

But, brother, she'd looked hot in that dress with her ruby lips and wavy hair....

Was she attached to someone else? For that matter, was he? On one hand, if he had a wife, hopefully she'd expect him to return to her and come looking for him when he didn't. The flip side was this pull toward Kinsey. If he had his phone he could do an online search of her

name and find out more about her. Frustrated
and bored, he went the old-fashioned route and
found a phone book in the drawer by the bed.
He just wanted to see her name, just to reas-
sure himself he hadn't made her up. There was
a map in the front of the book and he found her
street, Hummingbird Drive, curious as to how
far away she was. Not more than two or three
miles, he discovered, and for some reason, that
created a warmth in his heart where it had only
been cold before.

Hummingbird Drive. That's where a woman
like her should live, he decided. Someplace that
sounded as small and lovely and vibrant as she
was.

Feeling way too restless to stay in bed, he'd
pushed his IV stand around the looping corridors
right after Kinsey left and then again after dinner when the sedative they gave him had little
effect. He was supposed to spend a week here?
The idea made him crazy. But if things didn't
change, where exactly did he go next?

He finally decided to give sleep another
chance and settled back into the bed, but the
oblivion he'd so looked forward to continued to
elude him. Eventually, the hospital began qui-
eting down. A nurse gave him another pill, and
it was with relief when he felt his eyelids grow
heavy. He stirred sometime later, awoken by the

telltale swishing of the door that alerted him someone had entered his room.

He lay there for a second, expecting a cheery voice to announce it was time to check his blood pressure or take his temperature, but the room was eerily silent and the shadows too deep to make out a human shape.

"Who's there?" he asked.

The silence remained and Zane realized he must have woken up as someone left his room. Maybe a nurse had come in to take his vitals and found him sleeping soundly. Either that, or his drugged brain had created the noise.

Settling back against his pillow, he soon fell asleep again. This time he actually had a dream with substance. A wolf chased him through tall, golden grass. He panted from the effort to escape merciless fangs. And then suddenly, he was hanging from a tree, a noose around his neck. The tree was big and black with sprawling branches that scratched at the underbelly of the clouds. Its roots spread below him like an old man's hands clinging to the cracked earth. His neck hurt. He reached up to yank the rope away. He couldn't breathe.

His eyes finally opened but the nightmare didn't stop. A man stood over his bed, two big hands around Zane's neck. The pressure increased as the man pressed down harder and harder, grunting with the effort to strangle Zane who, between blankets and tubes, couldn't move. And he couldn't budge those merciless hands from their deadly grip, thumbs pressing into his windpipe.

The light suddenly went on. "Hey! What's going on?" a female voice yelled.

The hands instantly released Zane, who grabbed at his throat and gasped for air. He caught a glimpse of a man with shaggy white hair, horn-rimmed glasses and a bushy white mustache. The guy instantly turned toward the woman and pushed her hard. She went down amid a clatter of trays and equipment and the man disappeared out of the room.

Zane finally untangled himself and got out of bed. The nurse who had been knocked down struggled to sit up. He bent to help her just as an orderly arrived. "What are you doing to her?" the orderly demanded, trying to loosen Zane's grip on the nurse's arm.

"Tom, don't be silly, he's trying to help me," the nurse said as she finally got to her feet. She was a solidly built middle-aged woman with a no-nonsense approach. Her forehead was bleeding, but she paid it no attention. Fury raged in her eyes, but her expression changed to one of horror as she looked at Zane's throat. "Oh my gosh," she said. "That man was trying to choke you." She directed her next comment to the orderly. "Don't just stand there, Tom. Alert Security. Have them call the police."

The orderly took off back down the hall.

"The man who attacked you looked like Mark Twain," the nurse said as she blotted her forehead with a cloth. Her gaze dipped to Zane's neck again. You'd better get back into bed."

Zane shook his head and wished he hadn't when the room spun. "I think I'll sit for a while. I'm not anxious to lie down again."

"The stitches on your face look red. I'm calling the doctor right now."

"Please, I'm fine."

She pushed the intercom button that hung around her neck, speaking into the unit, asking for the doctor who showed up quickly and checked Zane over. He seemed to be about Zane's age, with fine blond hair and a boyish smile. He was the same doctor who'd checked on him earlier.

"Y'all are having yourself a heck of a day," the doctor said in a rich Southern drawl.

"That's one way of putting it."

"I'll stick a bandage on those stitches, just for the night. I don't think it needs to be redone. Open your mouth now, let's take a peek at your throat."

Zane did as ordered. He'd noticed his voice was deeper than it had been and his throat felt raw. "I'll prescribe some soothing spray," the doctor said. "Not much else we can do unless you want us to up the pain medication for a while."

"No," Zane said. "Thanks, anyway."

The doctor chuckled. "I took a look at all your X-rays. You have a fair number of healed breaks. Seems like you might lead quite an active life in some capacity. But you apparently mend well, so I suppose a little bitty concussion and a torn ligament or two won't be much of an obstacle to you."

The doctor left soon after. The nurse had yet to go tend to her own cut and hovered close by, obviously distressed that something like this had happened on her watch.

"I'll get your meds," she said at last.

"No, thanks. I don't want any more medicine."

"Did you know the man who tried to choke you?" she asked.

He gave her a look and she shook her head. "Sorry. I'm kind of rattled. For a second I forgot about the amnesia."

"Don't worry about it."

Detective Woods himself showed up a little later. He listened with narrowed eyes as Zane and the nurse related what they'd seen.

"Was he apprehended?" Zane asked at last.

"No one saw anyone who even vaguely resembled the man you two have described," Woods said. "We'll take a look at hospital video…" His voice trailed off as a security guard entered the room. He carried what looked like a white mop head in his hands.

"We found this on the second floor, stuffed in a trash can," he said, and Zane realized they were staring at a wig. "We also found one of them novelty masks, you know, the kind with the bushy eyebrows and glasses and a mustache. I put it in a paper bag for you." He now raised the bag proudly.

Woods snatched the bag away. "Next time just leave things where you find them and let us take care of it," he said. "I'll get someone to go check out that can, meanwhile, please make sure no one else touches it. And put the wig in another sack. I'll need to print you."

"I guess that explains the Mark Twain vibe," the nurse said as the guard left.

"And how he was able to leave the hospital without being noticed," Woods added.

The nurse, sporting a bandage on her forehead, insisted Zane climb back into bed. He met her gaze directly. "No," he said.

"You've had a traumatic event. I know the doctor said you'll be all right, but it's time for another sleeping tablet and you need to be in bed to take it."

"No more medicine," Zane said. He knew he was drawing a line in the sand but he'd had it.

"Really, sir."

"No, listen," Zane said. "You undoubtedly saved my life tonight. I'm very grateful to you and I promise to be a good patient starting tomorrow, but for right now, I need time to sit and digest everything that's happened and I don't want to be bothered by anything or anyone. I'm fine, the doctor said so. Go coddle someone who needs it, okay? Please?"

She produced a reluctant smile. "I'll check on you in a while."

He just nodded.

Woods shook his head as the swishing door behind the nurse sent chills racing down Zane's spine. His gaze dipped to Zane's neck and back to his face. "How are you feeling?"

"A little sore, a little confused, a little scared, to tell you the truth," Zane admitted. "And mad."

"I'm going to arrange to have Security post someone on your door. You'll be safe here."

Zane had heard that before. He gave a vague nod and waited until Woods had left the room, deep in thought but with a growing sense of conviction.

He knew what he had to do.

The closet Woods indicated earlier did indeed hold what was left of his clothing: two black boots, size eleven. That was it. Zane didn't know if his other clothes had been destroyed when he fell or confiscated by the police to search for fingerprints or some indication of the man who had attacked him on the street and stolen his identity, phone, what have you. He stuck the boots on right over the socks the hospital issued. After grabbing Woods's card and his own keys off his tray table, he opened the outside door.

The hall was clear except for a nurse engrossed in entering data into a computer mounted against the wall. Her back was to him. As quietly as he could, he pushed his IV stand the opposite direction, ignoring stiff, aching muscles and a headache he suspected would fell an ox. He'd seen a break room on one of his loops around the hospital floor and he made for that now.

His luck held. The room sported a table and chairs, a coffeemaker, fridge and microwave, but no people. He easily removed the IV from his arm and abandoned the stand in a corner. He found a pair of scrubs hanging on a hook and hastily put them on, adding a white lab coat that someone had left draped over the back of a chair. His keys and Woods's card went into the pocket. The hall was still empty. He knew the elevators were right across from the nurses' station so he used the stairwell, undoubtedly following the same path the man who had tried to choke him had taken an hour or two earlier. When he opened the door on the lobby floor, he half expected to find a security guard waiting for him, but the cavernous space was almost empty. A second later, he said good-night to the guard on duty at the exit and walked purposefully away from the hospital as though he did so every night of his life.

Was he really leaving without telling a soul where he was going? Was this what an innocent man did after a murder attempt?

What else was he supposed to do? Docilely lay back in his bed until his room was surrounded with police and security guards and he might as well tuck himself away in a jail cell?

No way. Depending on other people didn't sit well with him, not when the stakes were high and not when another gut feeling told him he knew how to take care of himself. It would be tricky defending himself against an unknown foe. Reason said that tonight was the culmination of something ongoing. He had no recollection of where he'd been or what he'd been doing. The killer would be back unless Zane managed to disappear until his memory returned, and that's just what he planned to do.

But where does a man without a penny, without an identity, without a friend in the world, actually go?

The keys jingled in his pocket as he walked and he took them out as he passed beneath a streetlight. Red Hot. A tractor dealership in Utah. Apparently no one had recognized his photograph. But maybe seeing a living breathing human being would be different.

If he remembered his geography, Utah was about four states away from New Orleans. A couple of thousand miles or so. It would take days to hitchhike there.

Well, it wasn't as though he had anything else to do, was it? He kept walking.

KINSEY STOOD ON the front porch of the house facing her mother, Frances. The abrupt door opening had caused her to stumble backward in her heels, and now she held on to a flaking post to steady her nerves.

What a day.

"Where have you been all night?" Frances demanded. "I called three times. Why are you all dressed up?"

Kinsey knew she and her mom shared certain similarities in appearance. Both were on the petite side, though Kinsey was a couple of inches taller, both curvy, both with deep brown eyes. Kinsey's hair was her natural shade of dark brown while Frances had dyed her hair her entire life. Currently reddish-brown, silver roots showed in the center part. Over sixty now, the years had started to show in the lines on her face and the sag in her shoulders. Kinsey had never understood why her mother settled for back-breaking, low-paying employment as she was well read and intelligent. Frances had stressed that no job was more or less noble than another.

Where they differed was internal: Kinsey open and curious, Frances suspicious and very much a mind-your-own-business woman. Kinsey artistic, sketching her way through life, as proficient at mixing paints as her mother was at whipping up pancake batter.

"We had a show," Kinsey said, deciding on the spot to skip the details about the bicycle and the cowboy. "Let's go inside."

"We better not," Frances said, softly closing the door behind her. She and Kinsey were now almost lost in shadows. Just a sliver of moonlight and the light filtering through a nearby window helped them see each other. "Bill is finally asleep," she added. "He's had a tough day and I don't want to chance waking him and get him coughing again."

"Were you waiting for me? I almost had a heart attack when the door opened like that."

"I was afraid you were *him*," Frances said, glancing behind Kinsey as though expecting someone else to materialize. Kinsey actually looked over her shoulder, but there was no one there that she could see. On the other hand, she couldn't see much.

"*Him* who?" she asked, her mind leaping straight to Ryan. Had he said or done something upsetting? What? What could he possibly say or do? "What's going on?"

"It's Bill's nephew, Chad. Bill got a note from

him saying that he was coming today or tomorrow. I've been on edge ever since reading it. Bill doesn't want him here."

"Oh, dear," Kinsey commiserated. She knew her mom didn't get along with Chad. "Can you call him and tell him that?"

"Neither Bill nor I know his phone number. I don't think he wants anyone to know how to reach him. That way, he can call all the shots. The last time he came, he accused me of stealing Bill's coin collection. He prowls around here making demands."

"Like what?"

"He wants me to show him all the things he remembers his uncle used to have, things like those coins and stamps and heaven knows what. And when he isn't taking inventory, he's eating, and guess who he expects to do all the cooking?"

"What can I do to help you?" Kinsey asked. For the life of her, she couldn't think of a darn thing.

Frances took a deep breath. "When I couldn't reach you, I called James Fenwick."

"Mr. Dodge's attorney?"

"Yes. You've met him."

"Guy about fifty, kind of stuffy?"

"I wouldn't describe him that way," Frances said. "He's been very kind to Bill. Lately he's been helping him go through his collection of books."

Kinsey could easily picture the room Mr. Dodge used as a bedroom. Every wall was covered with floor-to-ceiling shelves and each of those housed a wide array of books. She felt bad that she'd been less than flattering in her description of James Fenwick and now she mumbled, "That's very nice of him."

"Yes, it is. He's one of the few considerate people left on the planet. Anyway, Mr. Fenwick is out of town on business, but he'll come straight here when he drives home tomorrow. He said he'll leave before dawn."

"Good. What if I come by before work just to make sure things are okay until he gets here? Would that help?"

"Yes. Thank you. I know how busy you are."

"I wanted to ask you something, Mom," Kinsey added. "Do you know a woman named Sherry or Mary Smith?"

Her mother shook her head. "No. Why?"

There was no way in the world that Kinsey was going to add more stress to her mother. She omitted the fact that people had been asking about Bill Dodge's housekeeper—she'd tell her that tomorrow when the poor woman wasn't so overwhelmed. "No reason. I just heard the name."

Frances nodded. "Come early, okay? Bill is

better in the morning and always enjoys your visits. And heaven forbid, you don't want to run into Chad."

Though Kinsey had never met Mr. Dodge's nephew face-to-face, she did know his name was Chad Dodge. If her mother was any judge at all, Chad was a greedy, demanding man. Everyone knew he was set to inherit this house when Bill Dodge died, but apparently he wasn't content to wait.

Fatigue dragged at Kinsey as she agreed to be back bright and early in the morning. Her feet in the stacked-heel sandals hurt like blazes, her hair drooped down her sticky neck. Frances stepped back to ease open the front door and listen intently, her profile vivid in the stream of light flowing from within the house. Though still attractive, the years were taking a toll and Kinsey glanced away.

"I hear Bill coughing," Frances said. "I have to go."

"I'll see you tomorrow," Kinsey said. "Try not to worry too much."

Her mother slipped inside and closed the door behind her. Kinsey heard the slide of the dead bolt. It was a relief to collapse back into her car, start the air conditioner and polish off the now-tepid iced tea.

Fifteen minutes later, it was an even greater relief to turn onto Hummingbird Drive, a charming name for a decidedly ordinary-looking road. She pulled into her parking spot behind the house and got out, juggling the apple and banana she hadn't eaten yet, longing for the privacy of her own space in the apartment above the detached garage and the cool softness of her bed.

A voice from the shadows made her drop both pieces of fruit and she whirled around to find herself facing a large man. Even as she gasped, he moved into the light and she saw who it was.

With a hand on her chest, she blinked unbelieving eyes. "Zane?"

He had knelt to retrieve the fruit. "I didn't know for sure where you lived," he said softly as he straightened up. "I knocked at the main house, but no one is home."

"My landlord is up fishing in Alaska," she said. "My place is above the garage." She couldn't make sense of his being here. "Why aren't you in the hospital? You sound funny." She saw now that he wore hospital scrubs with a white lab coat. That didn't make any sense, either.

"I wasn't followed here," he said. "I made sure of that."

"Followed? What's going on? Wait, do you remember things about yourself?"

"No," he said. "No, that's not it." He looked directly into her eyes and her breath caught from his intense gaze that easily penetrated the dim light. "May I come inside for a few minutes?" he asked in that newly hoarse voice.

She wasn't sure what to do. It seemed insane to invite a stranger inside her home, especially one twice as big as she was. But she picked up no violent vibes directed her way. "I have to admit I'm curious about what's going on and why you're dressed like that, so I'll bite, come on in."

He followed her up the outside stairs and waited while she unlocked the flimsy little lock on her door, which, come to think of it, needed to be changed to a stronger one. When she turned to face him in the light of the room, she gasped again.

"What happened to your throat?" she asked, eyes wide.

He didn't answer immediately. His gaze seemed to fly around the room, from one wall to the next, one painted canvas after another, as though he couldn't quite take them all in at one time.

All those paintings in so little space probably came across as too much, but when you had a lot of paintings and limited wall space, they tended to add up.

"Did you create all of these?" he asked.

"Well, not the landscape, that's a Vincent van Gogh print, and the lilies are Monet…well, all the people, yes."

"You're amazing," he said, his gaze finally settling back on her face. "Who are all these people?"

She shrugged, unwilling to be distracted. "What happened to your neck?" she asked again.

He set the fruit on her table, then ran a hand through his hair. He seemed to exist in a perpetual state of sexy. It was just the way he was put together, the way he moved, his mannerisms and the expression in his eyes. But now bone-weary fatigue vied with that innate magnetism and seemed to win. "Mind if I sit down?" he asked.

"Help yourself," she said as she locked the front door.

He settled on her lime-green love seat. The apartment consisted of a kitchen/living area and a small bedroom/bath. Most of time it seemed pretty roomy, but Zane was at least six foot two and possessed a kind of commanding presence. She'd noticed this hours earlier when he stood on the sidewalk. "Would you like something cold to drink?" she offered as she started the electric fan in the window.

"Some water would be great," he said, and she fetched him a glass before perching on a counter stool.

After finishing his drink, he started in on his story. When he got to the part about waking up to find someone choking him, she almost fell off the stool.

"It has to be the same person as this afternoon," she said. "I'll never forget the brazen way he pushed you. Is the nurse okay?"

"She's fine."

"Thank heavens she came into your room." With a shudder, she added, "I can't believe you took out your own IV." She and needles were not the best of friends.

He rubbed his face with his hands as though trying to stay awake. It was the middle of the night by this time and she sympathized and shared his fatigue although his presence had driven most of hers away.

"And you have no idea what he looked like because of the disguise?"

He nodded. "That's right. Even his size was hard to gauge because it all happened so fast."

"But why did you leave the hospital? I don't get it. Woods told you he planned on posting a guard."

"I'm not entirely positive why I left," Zane said. "I guess I thought my chances were better on my own than being stuck in that place. Besides, what did I do to get in this kind of trouble? I'd kind of like to find that out before the police do. Anyway, I didn't know if they'd actually let me leave if I asked—I still don't know whose going to pay my bill, for instance. So I sneaked away and that's also more or less why I ended up at your house. I was going to borrow your phone and call Woods to try to explain, but I just decided against it."

"Why?"

"I guess I don't want him bugging you, and I don't want him trying to get me back into the hospital. He's a smart guy. He'll see my boots are gone and talk to the guard on duty and learn I walked away out of choice and he'll put two and two together. Maybe I'll call when I get out of town."

She nodded. His logic sounded reasonably sane to her. Well, at least as sane as escaping police protective custody to take your chances with a man who tried to kill you—twice.

"But I do need to borrow twenty dollars," he added. "I'll pay you back, I swear. If I'm going to hitchhike to Utah, I'm going to need something to eat along the way and I don't have a penny. Eventually I can probably hock my boots—well, anyway, how about it?"

"Of course," she said immediately. "The money is yours. And I'll pack you a lunch to take with you."

"That would be great. Thank you."

"Turkey on sour dough?"

"Anything you have," he said, "will be appreciated."

"I'm going to change clothes first, then I'll make you a lunch. Are you hungry now?"

"No."

Biting her lip, she added, "Zane, I should tell you that I found out why you had my name in your pocket. The grocer down the block from the gallery gave it to you because you were in the store asking about someone named Sherry or Mary Smith. Is there any chance that rings a bell?"

"None."

She hit her forehead with her palm. "Why didn't I think of the internet?" She retrieved her phone. A moment later, she shook her head. "Get this. There are over forty-seven million hits for Mary Smith." She tapped the tiny electronic keypad again. "Over six million for Sherry Smith. Without an age or a career or a location, it's impossible." She fooled around a little more with the search engine, typing Mary Smith, New Orleans, and the same for Sherry Smith. Nothing that appeared relevant in any way showed up.

"Well, Mr. Lee promised he'd call Detective Woods and tell him about your being in his store," she said with a sigh. She didn't mention the fact that she'd asked Mr. Lee to keep Bill Dodge and his housekeeper out of it because she felt guilty about that. Zane needed all the help he could get and she had no right to deny him the turning of every stone. She just needed some time to try to make sense of things.

She closed the bedroom door behind her and quickly slipped out of her clothes, exchanging the dress for shorts and a T-shirt. She left her feet bare, splashed water on her face and went back into the main room where she found Zane still staring at the paintings that surrounded him.

"Aren't you kind of warm in all those clothes?" she asked, and then felt her cheeks grow pink at the way those words could be taken.

He apparently didn't read anything in her voice but what was there—concern for his comfort. "No, I'm fine."

She sat down on the stool for a moment. "Zane, right after you asked about the Smith woman, you were hurt by an impulsive crazy person. I bet if we asked Woods where the real courier was robbed, it would turn out to be close to the grocery store. I think your attacker was in that store. Maybe he followed you." She stopped short of finishing the sentence—*or maybe you came in together.*

Was that possible?

"I was also hurt right after the grocer gave me your name," Zane said, smothering a yawn and apologizing for it. "I can't make sense of any of it and that's what's so frustrating."

"It'll come. I'll go make the sandwiches." She padded into the adjoining kitchen and got to work. She made him two generous sandwiches, found an ice pack in the freezer and a bottle of sweet tea in the refrigerator, included the apple and the banana she'd bought earlier and threw in a few granola bars for good measure. She'd been to the bank earlier that day so she knew she still had a couple of ATM twenties in her wallet.

When she turned to look back in the living room, she found Zane had fallen asleep with his head thrown back, his hands lying on the cushion next to his thighs, his legs sprawled in front of him as though he'd finally surrendered to his long, arduous day. His breathing seemed steady and deep and, without the impact of his gaze, he appeared wan and worn out. She bent to shake his shoulder and he turned slightly at her touch, his breath warm against her hand, but didn't waken.

Up close like this, the bruises on his throat looked like bloody fingerprints, red and ugly, grotesque in their cruelty and intent. A bright red dot of blood had seeped through the bandage over the stitches on his cheek.

She straightened up without touching him again, staring down at him for a moment, moved by his plight, touched by his decency and scared for his life. And totally intrigued.

How were they connected, where did her mother fit into this? Did Ryan have something to do with what happened? Could he have been the phony cyclist? She didn't think so, but was she positive?

No answers, not tonight, anyway. She quietly put the bag of food in the refrigerator, dimmed the lights and with one last look at the gorgeous man asleep on her love seat, closed the bedroom door behind her.

Five minutes later, she slept.

Chapter Four

The sun was just peeking in the window when Zane sat up straight. The room did a one-eighty and he grabbed his head as he blinked a few times. Where in the hell was he?

The dozens of pairs of eyes staring endlessly from the paintings covering the walls brought the last few hours crashing back like a rogue wave on a beach. Unfortunately, that's all that came back. His mind was still as empty as a purloined vault. It looked as if his loss of memory wasn't the overnight variety.

He glanced at the closed bedroom door behind which he imagined Kinsey slept, turning suddenly when a noise at the front door jarred him fully awake. He was on his feet and ready for action when Kinsey let herself inside, stopping abruptly when she saw his aggressive stance.

"Sorry," he said, relaxing his muscles. "I guess I'm a little jumpy." It was the first time he'd spoken since waking. His voice was as raspy as it had been the night before and each word seemed to rake the inside of his throat.

"You didn't wake up when I left," she explained, the alarm fading from her eyes. Dressed in a cool blue wispy blouse and white pants, she looked as though she belonged on top of a mountain or in a meadow or something. He could only imagine what he looked like.

"I went out to buy coffee at the little place on the corner," she said as she offered him a twelve-ounce container with a heady aroma. "I thought you might appreciate a cup. I'm afraid I have to be at my mother's place in thirty minutes, which means we have to leave here pretty soon."

With heartfelt thanks, he accepted the proffered coffee and took a deep whiff as he slipped off the plastic sipping lid. She sat down on a nearby chair and stared at him a few seconds. "How are you feeling? How's your throat?"

"I'll live," he said.

"I hate to say this, but those bruises look worse today than they did last night. And the abrasions on your forehead and cheek…well, anyway, it might be hard to win the trust of a Good Samaritan who gets little more than a glimpse to form an opinion of you."

"You're referring to motorists who might be going my way?"

"Yes."

He touched his neck. Neither the scrubs nor

the lab coat he'd filched from the hospital had a collar he could use to conceal the marks his attacker had left. "I don't have much choice," he said. "Speaking of that, do you think you could drop me off close to the interstate on your way to your mother's house? It might be easier to hitch a ride from there. I'll stand somewhere where people can get a good long look at me and sense what a stalwart fellow I am."

"I have an idea," she said, leaning forward. "Let me loan you the money for a bus ticket."

Nothing about her, from her old car to this barely furnished apartment to the decent but inexpensive clothes on her back, suggested Kinsey was rolling in dough. "That's okay," he said softly. "I don't want to go further in debt. The twenty you're going to loan me will get me by."

She nodded, perhaps relieved but too nice to show it. She took a sip of her coffee and spoke again. "I have something I have to tell you," she said, sliding him a nervous glance.

"Is there time? Shouldn't we be leaving?"

"Yes, but you have to know this. Remember last night when I told you the man at the grocery store was going to call Detective Woods and tell him that you'd been in that day asking about a woman?"

"Sure," he said.

"What I didn't tell you was that he said you also asked about an elderly man in the neighborhood. Specifically, you asked about this man's housekeeper."

"I wonder what that was about," he said, noting the way she avoided his gaze and clutched the paper cup in her hands. Finally, she looked at him again. "I asked Henry, he's the grocer, not to tell the police about the housekeeper."

"Why?"

"Because she's my mother."

He set his cup down on the chest Kinsey used as a coffee table. "I don't quite understand," he said.

"And I don't have time to explain," she said, her expression worried now. "Anyway, Henry said you asked about the housekeeper right after you asked about Smith. I mentioned this to my mother last night and she claims she's never heard of anyone with that name and I believe her, but that's why you had my name. Henry either knows Mom and I are related or thinks we're friends. He gave you my name to get you out of his store because you were holding up the line and he needed to break up a fight over a box of beignet mix."

Zane stared at her a minute. Was this for real? It sounded like something out of an old sitcom. "Okay," he said at last. "So all that happened, but why can't your mother just tell Detective Woods what she told you, she doesn't know the woman, end of conversation."

"You don't know my mother," Kinsey said.

"Obviously."

"And I don't have time to try to explain her now." She glanced at her watch, and stood abruptly. "It's getting late," she said as her phone rang. She dug into the small purse she wore across her body and emerged with the cell phone. She scanned the caller screen impatiently and he thought he saw disappointment on her face. The look disappeared as she hit a button and slipped the device back in her bag. "That means you have to go, too. I can't leave you here—"

"I know," he said as he stood. His body screamed in protest at the abrupt action, reminding him of what he'd been through fewer than twenty-four hours before. "Do we have enough time for me to splash some cold water on my face?" he managed to say, his voice more hoarse than ever.

"Of course," she said.

At her bedroom door, he turned. "I'd like to go with you to your mother's place."

"No way," she said, her attention back on the phone.

"Kinsey, think about it. Maybe your mother knows me or of me. Maybe that's why I asked about her. Or how about the guy she works for? Maybe one of them will recognize me, give me a name and a family, an identity."

"That's not likely," Kinsey said, shaking her head.

"But it's the only lead besides that tractor dealership in Utah. I have to try."

Her nod seemed reluctant. He continued on his way before she could change her mind.

THE CALL HAD BEEN from Marc. It wasn't uncommon for her boss to call her with a short list of errands to perform when she opened the gallery, but right now that prospect didn't interest her.

Ryan still hadn't returned her call. She'd looked up his company's number before leaving for the coffee that morning and programmed it into the phone. The original plan had been to call after she dropped Zane off by the interstate, but his announcement that he was going all the way with her nixed that.

She punched in the New York number now. It was answered on the first ring by an actual human being, which seemed amazing considering it was a Saturday morning. The greeting was breezy but followed by a long pause when Kinsey asked for Ryan Jones. The man on the phone finally said, "Would you repeat that name?"

Kinsey did, with the explanation that Ryan was in New Orleans that weekend working on their levee project.

Another pause. "I'm sorry," the man said. "I don't know anyone named Ryan Jones."

"He's one of your engineers," she protested.

"I'm actually the owner of this business," he explained. "I came in early today to work on… well, you don't care about that. Listen, we're not all that big an operation, so I know every one of my employees. There is no one here named Ryan Jones."

Kinsey thought for a second. "Maybe he's with your New Orleans section."

"What New Orleans section? We don't have one."

"You have no contracts down here at all?"

"None. I'm afraid someone has given you false information."

"Is there another A and P Engineering firm in New York?"

"No," he said gently. "Just this one. I'm sorry."

"One more thing. Do you know someone named Ryan Jones in another capacity, like a neighbor or someone at a club or maybe a business associate, you know, something like that?"

He seemed to think for a few seconds. "No," he finally said. "Sorry."

Kinsey murmured something and clicked off the phone, glancing up when Zane cleared his throat. He took one look at her face and moved toward her. "Are you okay?" he asked.

She stared into his crystal-blue eyes. Ryan had lied to her about his job and probably everything else. He'd asked questions about her mother and then he'd disappeared right around the same time that Zane took the stage. But it hadn't been Ryan who had pushed Zane—she was almost positive of that, even though she hadn't seen the attacker's face. Ryan was too tall to be that man and he didn't move in the same way.

So perhaps Ryan was Zane's adversary. Or were they in cahoots? If so, in what capacity and most important, why did her mother seem to be in the middle of it? She pulled up the pictures she'd taken, almost all of paintings she'd admired or people whose faces had intrigued her. She finally found what she was looking for, a photo of a painting of the Mississippi River. She'd taken the picture at a street show a few weeks before. Ryan had walked into the frame and she'd inadvertently caught his profile.

She handed the phone to Zane. "Does this man look familiar to you? Could he have been the man in the hospital, for instance?"

Zane studied the image for a second. "I can't tell. You think he's connected to me?"

"I don't know. Maybe," she answered honestly as she took her car keys from her bag.

"Is he someone important?"

She shook her head. "I don't know that, either."

KINSEY PULLED UP in front of the garish Victorian and parked behind a blinding-white luxury sedan. She had a feeling Bill Dodge's attorney had arrived at the house first and couldn't help wondering in what shape she would find her mother.

"This is some house," Zane said as he looked around.

"Yeah."

"It doesn't really fit the neighborhood anymore, does it?"

"Not really," Kinsey said, but she was distracted. Nerves and trepidation made her throat dry. "The land it's sitting on is the real value."

"I bet," Zane said.

They'd climbed the rickety stairs by now and Kinsey grabbed Zane's arm. "Do me a favor, okay?"

"Anything."

"Just go along with whatever story pops into my head to explain the fact you're in hospital scrubs."

"What are you going to say?"

"I haven't the slightest idea," she admitted. Maybe they should come up with a plan. She was about to suggest this when the door opened and they found themselves face-to-face with an average-sized man in his midfifties with perfectly styled graying hair. He held a briefcase in one hand. They caught him midsentence and he stopped talking at once.

"Hello, Mr. Fenwick," Kinsey said.

"Kinsey, you're looking well." James Fenwick's gaze left her face immediately and traveled up to Zane's. Kinsey had called him dour the night before, but now she looked at his tanned skin and the expectant smile curving his lips and he seemed a little less formidable than he had before.

Kinsey's mother was right behind Fenwick. She, too, looked at Zane, but instead of curiosity, her expression reflected fear. As long as Kinsey had been aware of her mother's emotional state of being, meeting strangers was always fraught with this initial reaction of distrust.

"Who is this?" Frances Frost demanded, narrowing her eyes and frowning. "What's wrong with his neck?"

"I had a riding accident yesterday," Zane explained as his hand flew to his throat. "While playing polo. Anyway, my horse's flying hooves almost took my head off." As Kinsey gaped at this explanation, Zane cleared his throat. "You look familiar. Have me met before, Mrs. Frost?"

"No," she said firmly. "I've never seen you before right now. Your clothes…are you a doctor?"

"Yes," he said easily. "Yes, I am."

"What are you doing here with Kinsey?"

"Zane is a neighbor," Kinsey said. "He needed a ride to work this morning."

Frances waved all this aside. "Come with me," she told Zane. "Bill's cough is worse. He won't let me call his doctor, but since you're a doctor and you're here anyway, you can take a look at him."

"Now, Frances," James Fenwick said gently, "this young man isn't Bill's doctor. Bill's situation is too serious to fool around with, you know that."

"Yes, I do know that. But Bill's doctor isn't here and this man is." Kinsey could tell her mother was digging in her heels.

"I don't have any...equipment," Zane said, "but I'll be happy to talk to him if it will make you feel better."

The two of them disappeared inside the house.

"Your mother is a woman of strong conviction," Fenwick said.

"You mean she's stubborn."

"Not a bad trait in this day and age when everyone rolls over." He seemed to smile at Kinsey's mom's quirks. "Is your friend really a doctor? I didn't want to say anything, but it looks as though he slept in his scrubs and he hasn't shaven. What's his name? Zane what?"

"Doe," Kinsey said. "Zane Doe. And he looks a little worn-out because he worked half the night and has to go back and his shower was broken." She stopped herself before throwing in any more made-up details. "So, Mr. Fenwick, have you talked to Bill and my mother about

Bill's nephew's impending visit? They were both pretty upset about it yesterday."

"I did talk to them," Fenwick said as he checked his watch. "I'm going to have to run. I have a meeting in thirty minutes. Don't worry about your mother. She'll call me the moment Chad appears and I'll be back here within fifteen minutes. I won't allow that rascal to make trouble, I promise you that."

"I know you're good to Bill," Kinsey said.

"Yes," he said, and then added in a soft voice, "And I don't like to see Frances upset. She's a special lady."

Flabbergasted, Kinsey nodded.

"Well, nice to see you, Kinsey, take care, say goodbye to your mother for me, will you?"

Kinsey nodded again. As she crossed the porch, she heard Fenwick's car door slam. The sound of his revving engine followed her inside.

She found everyone in the den that Bill Dodge now used as his bedroom. The walls were still lined with row upon row of books, though there were also signs that sorting had begun. Kinsey knew from the times she'd studied the spines that just about every area of interest was covered. Many small libraries would like to have such collections.

Bill had mounted her Christmas gift to him on a prize piece of wall real estate, one of the few empty spots to be found. It was a painting

Kinsey had done using an old photograph of Mr. Dodge back when he fished the river. In it, he wore a hat punctured by dozens of fishing flies and he carried a pole, but she'd also tucked a small book into his breast pocket with only the word *Huckleberry* showing. Kinsey felt very honored that he liked the painting so much.

"There's my girl," Bill said as she entered the room. "Frances was just going to get me and the good doctor a cup of herbal tea. Sit down here and keep me company while she's gone."

The pictures on the wall showing him standing next to various dignitaries through the years revealed Bill Dodge had once been a tall man with hair as dark as Zane's was now. Time and illness had softened all the edges, wrinkled his skin and faded his vibrancy.

None of that affected the kindness of his expression. Having never known her father and growing up with a paucity of adult men in her life, Kinsey enjoyed the way Bill Dodge doted on her. She sat by his chair, marveling that anyone who looked so frail could project so much curiosity. His freckled skull sported few hairs, his eyebrows had all but disappeared, but the lively depths of his blue eyes revealed an active mind and inquisitive nature. She knew he'd started his adult life as a fireman, retired from that, went to college, became a teacher and then graduated from that into real estate before running for city council. He'd been a major influence in one small pocket of New Orleans's history. He'd fished, sailed, bound books and dabbled in glass blowing. In short, he'd been quite the Renaissance man.

"I'll help with the tea," Zane offered.

Frances tried to wave him away, but he blithely pretended he didn't know what she was doing and followed her from the room.

"Are you terribly upset about your nephew coming for a visit?" Kinsey asked, not really trusting her mother's take on the situation. Frances regarded a door-to-door salesman as an interloper. A houseguest must really annoy her.

"Well, you see," Bill said, pausing to cough into a handkerchief. Her mother and Mr. Fenwick were right, the cough sounded ominous. "I hadn't seen Chad in years and years when he showed up here and tried playing the doting nephew." More coughs racked his frail body and Kinsey put out a hand to grip his shoulder. He put his head back down on the pillow and closed his eyes.

"He's your sister's son, right?" she said, hoping to do all the talking so he wouldn't have to. "Mom said she was almost a generation younger than you and that after she died, her husband moved away with their son."

"He came for visits…once in a while," Bill said. He opened his eyes. "I have something for you." He gestured toward the far wall. "Package in the top drawer of that old chest. Fetch it for me."

Kinsey did as he asked, finding what he wanted tucked away under clothes she'd never seen him wear. She handed it to Mr. Dodge before reclaiming her seat. "Why are we whispering?" she asked.

"Because I want to give you this without your mother around," he said as he presented the tissue-wrapped package back to Kinsey.

"Why?" Kinsey asked as she took it.

"I don't want to get into an argument with James Fenwick. Just not strong enough to fight all of them. He insists we catalogue everything. And if anyone tells Chad that I'm giving things away, he'll turn more belligerent than ever. He's got quite the temper. Best I just do what I want without anyone throwing in their two cents."

This long speech seemed to have exhausted him again. Kinsey suspected that he'd probably given away the coin collection that Chad accused her mother of stealing. Kinsey instinctively felt her mother could fight her own battles and that Bill Dodge was the one who deserved to live the rest of his life in whatever way he wanted.

"Do you think Mom rats on you to your lawyer?" she asked.

"Of course not," he scoffed, and then coughed

again. To Kinsey's untrained ears, the cough sounded deep and disturbing and she suddenly understood her mother grabbing onto Zane when she was told he was a doctor. "But I know she occasionally confides in him," Bill added with a wheeze. "She could mention the fact I've been giving my books to special friends and then Fenwick would start in. I don't have an argument in me. Go ahead, unwrap it."

Touched by the very fact he was bestowing an obviously important possession to her, she lifted the tissue to find a small five-by-seven-inch book with gold-leaf writing on the cover. Kinsey ran her fingers over the embossed title as she read it aloud, *"Female Artists of the Twentieth Century."* She opened the pages to find reproductions of works and biographies of artists she'd both heard of and never knew existed. The edges of the paper were gilded while the binding was constructed of spectacular red leather embossed with tiny artists' pallets. "This is beautiful," she said, raising her gaze to meet Bill Dodge's. He smiled with joy. "Thank you, Mr. Dodge. I'll treasure this."

"You'll be in the next edition if they make one," he said. "Front and center, Kinsey Frost, portraitist extraordinaire." They heard footsteps approaching and he added, "Tuck it in your handbag now. Our secret. Man my age needs a secret or two."

Kinsey hastily closed the book and squeezed it into her small cross-body bag as Bill leaned close with a couple more whispered questions. "Is that young man really a doctor?"

Kinsey shook her head. "How did you know?"

"I've been around a lot of doctors lately. Why is he dressed like he is?"

"He has no other clothes," she said and wondered what Bill would make of that comment.

"So he's in trouble," Bill stated.

She nodded.

He sat up straighter as the other two entered the room. "Took you long enough," he said, but the comment was followed by an attack of coughing that brought Frances racing to his side.

"No offense to you, Doctor," she said to Zane, "but I don't think Mr. Dodge's cough has a thing to do with allergies like you said. I'm calling Bill's real doctor."

"That's a good idea," Zane said as Frances left the room. He looked at Bill and added, "Sorry, sir, but she's right, you know."

Bill's eyes were watering. His breathing sounded ragged and his face was pale.

"I suppose she'll do what she wants anyway," Bill said. Zane asked to use a bathroom and Kinsey told him where it was. As soon as he left, Bill caught Kinsey's hand in his. His voice had withered considerably and now the whisper didn't seem so much a choice as a necessity. "Go back to that same dresser…bottom drawer…jeans, shirts…you know, for your friend. About his size…once upon a time. Take what you want… I won't need them…again."

"Thank you," Kinsey said and did as he requested. The clean clothes were all neatly folded and she haphazardly chose several items and stacked them on a chair. The long dialogue had wiped Bill out and she helped him sit up in bed to ease his breathing.

Eventually her mother arrived. "The doctor said to call an ambulance and take him to the hospital. He'll meet us there."

The next half hour passed in a blur. Zane disappeared with some of the clothes and returned looking informal but spectacular in faded jeans and a black shirt. They stowed the rest of the items in a small satchel that Frances pointed out during one of her trips between the front door and Bill's bedside. She completely ignored the fact that Zane had morphed from a crumpled "doctor" to a regular guy.

"I feel funny leaving my mother in the lurch," Kinsey told Zane. "I'd better drive her to the hospital and stay with her until Bill is safe."

"Yes, of course," Zane said.

"I can drop you off."

"I'd appreciate that. The hospital isn't far from the highway, is it?"

"No."

"Then just take me there and I'll walk over."
He looked straight into her eyes. The power of
all that dazzling blue made her heart race. "This
means goodbye."

"Not the way I wanted," she said. She hated
any goodbye, there had been far too many in
her life, but this one, done prematurely and in
haste, really sucked. "Be careful," she added.
"Let me know when you remember who you
are. Promise me."

"I promise," he said, his fingers grazing her
cheek.

They were alone except for Bill, whose eyes
were closed. Kinsey was surprised and yet not
surprised when Zane leaned down and touched
her lips with his. Her racing heart almost exploded.

"Just as ripe and juicy as I knew they would
be," he whispered, and kissed her briefly again.
They stepped apart as the sound of the ambulance siren exploded into their consciousness.

THEIR NEXT GOODBYE was done on the run. Kinsey was spared watching Zane walk away as
her mother propelled her into the hospital. They
found seats in the waiting room. While Frances tapped her foot and sighed repeatedly, Kinsey found a corner and called Marc, explaining
where she was and that she might not make it
in to work at all.

"No problem," he told her. "Violet and Brent can cover for you. We'll see you when we see you."

"It might be a few days."

"Like I said, no problem."

Kinsey looked at her mother as she walked back to her seat. Her mother's gaze was fixed on the closed steel doors of the emergency room. She looked as frightened as she did worried and, for the first time, Kinsey wondered if it ever occurred to her mom that when Bill died, she'd be out of work and a home. Of course, it must have. It would hardly be the first time one of her jobs ended and she had to start over again. How did she do it?

After four hours of endless waiting interspersed with occasional assurances that things were progressing and they should be patient, a doctor finally appeared and explained that Bill's condition had stabilized but he wanted to keep him overnight. Frances could see him once they transferred him upstairs.

Kinsey was preparing herself for an all-night waiting-room vigil when the door blew open and James Fenwick appeared. He pocketed the cell phone he'd been holding to his ear. "I've just heard, I've been in and out of meetings," he said, grasping Frances's elbows. "Is he okay?"

She explained what they had learned and he assured her that he was there to stay. When she expressed concern about Bill's nephew arriving to an empty house, Fenwick shook his head. "The place is locked, right? If he finds his way in, so be it. We'll worry about Chad when we have the time. Okay?"

Frances slumped against James as she nodded. She appeared close to tears. Kinsey was about to offer comfort when Fenwick's arm stole around her mother's shoulder and he squeezed her. She smiled up at him and in that instant, Kinsey knew her mother had finally created a family of sorts that didn't require Kinsey's total attention. The thought was amazing: a little sad in a weird way, and joyous in a hundred others. It seemed a trumpet should blare or confetti should fall— something, anything, to mark this totally unaddressed but major transformation. Hallelujah.

Kinsey touched her mom's arm and got a distracted glance. "Oh, Kinsey. James is here."

"I see that," Kinsey said.

"You can leave if you have other obligations," Fenwick said. "Your mother won't be alone."

"I know you're incredibly busy," her mother said. "There must be a million things you need to do. Don't worry about me."

"Okay," Kinsey said. "Tell Bill not to scare me like that again, okay?"

"I will. And thank you for sitting here with me so long."

"I love you, Mom."

The two older people declared their intention to find the cafeteria for a late lunch before going to Bill's room. Kinsey declined the offer to join them and, feeling lighter than she had in so long she couldn't remember, left the emergency room.

And then she remembered that Zane was gone, this time for good.

Chapter Five

Zane's left leg throbbed. When he'd changed into Mr. Dodge's old clothes, he'd found bruises from his knee on up. That made sense, considering he'd landed on that side when he was flung into the street. But now, between walking and standing so long, his endurance was spent.

What was taking so long? Maybe he should move on to plan B.

Instead, he found a nearby patch of green and lowered himself onto the grass, using a landscape rock to lean against. Not bad, he thought, better than standing with nothing to look at but pavement and cars. The sun felt good on his battered cheek, seemed to sink down under his skin and massage the dull ache in his head and the wounded nerves of his neck and shoulders. He closed his eyes and tried to think positive thoughts.

He must have dozed, for suddenly he was awake and looking up at the only face on the planet he wanted to see.

Kinsey's eyes were huge as she studied him. "What are you doing here at the hospital? You should be all the way out of Louisiana by now."

He got to his feet as gracefully as he could manage. "I couldn't leave," he said, brushing himself off. He'd moved too fast and his head spun. Kinsey shot out an arm to steady him and he winced. "How is Bill?"

"Holding his own," she said. "Have you been out here all this time?"

"Yeah. I started walking back to the highway and then I suddenly knew I had to make sure you didn't need help before I left. You've done so much for me."

She smiled, hugged him briefly and stepped back. That brief hug was the first time she'd put her arms around his torso, the first time she'd been that close to the strong maleness of his whole body, and she was suddenly burning with awareness. "Why didn't you come inside? Why stay out here where it's hot and sultry?"

"That particular hospital holds some unpleasant memories for me. I like being outside better."

She opened her car. "Get in, I'll give you a lift to the road." Eventually, she merged into the far-right lane. "Remember, you promised to let me know when you figure out who you are," she said as the on-ramp approached.

"Pull over to the side of the road," he said. "No reason for you to go any farther. I can walk up the ramp." He hoped his voice didn't reveal how reluctant he was to leave her side. Hot pangs of loss ate away at his stomach as he grabbed the bag with all the grub she'd fixed him the night before, and turned back for a last look at her. To him she always seemed full of light and now he realized she was achingly familiar in a way no other person was. He fought the idea that it wasn't just because he could remember no one else. It was her. "Here I am thanking you again," he said and hoped she blamed his thick voice on his battered throat. "I don't know what I would have done without you."

"Another goodbye," she whispered. "Our third or fourth."

He was surprised to hear in her voice the same longing he felt inside, to belong, to connect. "Then we won't say goodbye this time," he said.

She reached across the space between them with both hands and gently turned his collar up. "That looks better," she whispered. "Good luck. Be careful."

"You, too," he said.

A smile trembled on her lips. Her lips, the same succulent red lips that had been driving him crazy since the first moment he laid eyes on her.

This time, she was the one who initiated a kiss, but this one wasn't quite as chaste as earlier. This one echoed the same notes of longing her voice had contained and he responded to it at once.

She couldn't know how much he had anticipated this moment when they kissed for real, she couldn't possibly guess at the thunderclap her lips set loose in his brain. He kissed her back, again and again, lost in the gentle but blinding tension, the noise in his head deafening him to everything.

What was he doing? He had to act now or he'd chicken out. He tore himself away from her and all but threw himself out of her small car. The door slammed closed behind him as, without another word, he purposefully put one foot in front of the other, not looking back, not daring to linger.

KINSEY SAT IN the car and watched Zane's retreat. Her lips still burned. Damn, that man tasted and kissed just as good as she'd known he would.

Did he realize that he limped? Did he have any idea how the past events had compromised his voice and his endurance? He hadn't mentioned a thing about the vicious attempts on his life; surely he hadn't dismissed them.

But what if he had? What if the man who had tried to kill him had been watching them all morning?

Don't be crazy, she scolded herself. Zane had been a perfect target in the parking lot for hours.

He'd slept through her approach. If she'd been the bad guy, he'd be dead.

Unless the parking lot was too public for something like that. What if he was biding his time? What if he sat nearby right now, in one of the cars parked right over there or hovering unseen in the traffic behind her? What if he was just waiting for her to pull away and then he would pick up Zane. And Zane, who had never seen the man's face, would climb in to meet his doom. That would be it, third time's a charm, the culprit could be successful.

The premonition was too great to ignore. She put the car in gear. As she drove up the ramp, she checked her rearview mirror. Every other car now seemed to hold a predator. At the sound of her approaching engine, Zane turned with his thumb out. He looked startled when they made eye contact and she slowed down. He opened the passenger door and stared at her.

"What—"

"Get in," she said.

"But—"

"There's a truck coming. Please, just get in."

He did as she asked and she sped up as the truck whizzed around her while blaring its horn.

"Kinsey, what are you doing?" Zane asked.

"I'm driving you to Utah." She darted him a glance. "You're in no shape to hitchhike. There are coated aspirin in the glove box and a bottle of water in with your food unless you drank it already."

"I have some left," he said. He found the medicine and shook three out into his hand. After he swallowed them he stared at her. "Be honest with me. Are you doing this because of our kisses?"

"No," she scoffed. "Good heavens, I'm not fourteen."

He sighed impatiently and she took the hint and started talking. "You were asking about my mother before you were pushed into the street. What you don't know is that my boyfriend of sorts was also asking about my mother that same afternoon on that same street."

"You have a boyfriend?"

"A sort of boyfriend. Except now I find that he isn't what he said he was."

"How does he explain himself?"

"Who knows? He isn't answering my calls."

After a lengthy pause, he sighed. "If my head didn't hurt so much, I'd shake it in befuddlement."

"There's a connection of some kind, I mean, between you and the man I know as Ryan Jones. At least I think there is. And my mother, of all people, seems to be at the epicenter of it all."

"So that's why you're driving me to Utah. Listen, why don't you just foot me a bus ticket like you offered. Sooner or later, my memory will return and I'll pay you back."

"Is the thought of my company for a couple of days really so terrible?" she asked with a quick glance.

"You know it's not that," he said. "This is just too big a commitment considering…everything."

"But it's not, Zane, that's what I'm trying to tell you. Somehow I feel that your destiny is entwined with mine. Let me come with you."

"What about your job?"

"The gallery doesn't have anything major planned for two weeks. Marc will be okay, I'm not his only employee. Besides, I just have to do this. I have to protect my mother."

"By leaving her all alone in New Orleans?"

Kinsey shook her head. "Mr. Fenwick seems kind of attentive."

He rubbed his forehead without comment.

"You have to understand," she added. "I spent most of my life in very close contact with my mother and there were no men allowed. Zero, zilch. I thought it was because she'd been so devastated by my father's death that she'd sworn off love."

"How did he die, Kinsey?"

"In a bus crash up in Maine. He was coming home from a construction job. His body was burned beyond recognition. Mom said they had to use dental records to identify him. It took a few weeks, so the accounts all list him as un-identified. That seemed like a terrible injustice when I was a kid. Anyway, she finally agreed to take me to the site when I was about fourteen. I'm not sure what I expected to find all those years later, just some kind of remembrance for my dad and the other ten people who died that day. But, of course, there was no trace of the tragedy." Her heart flip-flopped in her chest. Was she still holding on to that moment of child-ish disappointment?

"I'm sorry," he said gently.

She smiled. "It all happened a long time ago. I built him up in my head—there were so few mementos of him, as though Mom couldn't bear to be reminded—anyway, and now here she is acting coy with another man. It's a little jarring."

"Does it bother you?"

"No. It's her life. She deserves to live it after devoting so many years to me." She sighed and added, "That's enough about my history."

"Well, we sure as hell won't have much of a conversation if we depend on what I know of my past to keep us occupied," he said.

She cast him a thoughtful look. "How does it feel to leave New Orleans? Like a giant weight is being lifted from your shoulders?"

She saw him shrug and it looked good on him, just the way everything else did. A shrug called

attention to his shoulders and they looked outstanding encased in the black cotton of his new-
to-him shirt. Add the self-deprecating smile that
lit his eyes until they glimmered with blue light
and she was mesmerized. "Not really," he said.
"In a way, leaving feels like I'm abandoning the
only sliver of history I possess." After a deep
sigh, Zane's fingers braised her thigh. "Correc-
tion. It feels like I'm abandoning half the bits of
history. You're the other half and you're here,
and okay, I admit it, I'm glad."

"Good," she said.

"And with any luck, we're leaving a would-
be killer behind."

"Hmm…" she murmured, recalling how
spooked she'd been when she'd watched him
walk away.

"What's he look like?" Zane asked.

"Who?"

"Your sort of boyfriend."

"Tall like you, curly blond hair, brown eyes."
She sighed and added, "Enough about me. I'm
starving. Is there any food left in that sack?"

"One sandwich," he said, digging into the bag
and producing it.

"Want to share it with me?" she asked as he
unwrapped it for her.

"No, I ate mine an hour or two ago. Then I
ate the apple and the banana. This sandwich
is yours."

As she drove and munched, she noticed Zane's head nodding and encouraged him to get comfortable and close his eyes. "The fastest way to get to Utah from here is to travel up through Shreveport, over to Dallas, and then on to Albuquerque. St. George, Utah, is about a hundred miles northeast of Las Vegas. It's going to take over twenty-four hours of driving."

"How do you know all this?"

"We traveled around a lot when I was growing up. Now, get some sleep, okay?"

He finally did as she suggested, and for over three hours, Kinsey drove in peace and quiet. She just hoped it wasn't the kind of peace and quiet that precedes a storm.

ZANE WOKE UP when the car stopped. He looked around as he blinked himself into full consciousness. Kinsey had pulled into the parking lot of a wood-shingled joint promising the best barbecue in Louisiana. Judging from the enticing aromas adrift on the very faint breeze, it might actually turn out to be the truth.

"Feel better?" she asked him.

"Yeah, thanks for the nap," he said. "Where are we?"

"On the other side of Shreveport. You slept through the worst traffic, but I'm hungry again and I need to walk around. I thought we could get something to eat and then hit the road again."

"Sounds good."

The restaurant was bustling and the bar area was filled with people having a raucous time. After the quiet of the past twenty-four hours, this assault of noise and color and vibrancy actually felt good to Zane. After freshening up, they were told to choose a table and found a small booth located near a window.

Kinsey ordered half a rack of ribs and sketched on the back of the throwaway menu while awaiting delivery of their food. The image of their waitress began to emerge, then the bartender's with the handlebar mustache. Next, with just a few strokes, she captured the images of three men sitting at the bar.

"Who are all those people in the paintings hanging on your walls?" he asked.

"Just people. Faces I saw, people like that bartender and our waitress. A few of them were friends from when I was younger. I went through a stage of looking at old school pictures and then attempting to age people to see what they would look like now."

Their dinner finally arrived and Kinsey attacked it with gusto. His throat wasn't quite up to that yet—the sandwich had been hard enough to get down. He settled on sides of soft food that presented fewer challenges, but he got a kick out of her obvious pleasure with the ribs. The amusement suddenly turned into something else when she licked sauce off her fingertips. He found the sight of her tongue teasing her lips spellbinding.

"What's wrong?" she asked.

"Not a thing."

"Why are you looking at me like that?" She switched to a Wet Wipe to finish the cleanup. It was more efficient but not nearly as entertaining.

"I've become obsessed with your lips," he confessed. She didn't say anything for a minute and he wondered if he'd alarmed or offended her.

Then those wonderful lips curved into a smile. "I love your eyes."

"Really?"

"Your mouth isn't bad, either."

They stared at each other for a long, quiet moment until the tension between them burned Zane's skin. He had no memory of his character, of what kind of man he was, although he was willing to bet he was a one-woman kind of guy. His body was telling him Kinsey was that one woman. She wasn't only real because she was damn near the only person he knew; she was real because he could feel her inside his bones. "Too bad you have a sort of boyfriend," he finally said.

"Too bad you might have a wife and half a dozen kids," she countered.

"On the other hand, your sort of boyfriend

has disappeared, right? And even if I am married in real life, right now, in my head and heart, I'm free."

When her eyes narrowed and she frowned, he gently stroked the back of her hand. "I'm just joking around, Kinsey. Don't look so worried."

"It's what you just said about Ryan," she said, leaning forward. "I've been assuming he's been avoiding me. But now that I think of it, Marc said Ryan left in a hurry after getting a phone call. As far as I know, that's the last anyone saw of him. What if the same person who's been attacking you attacked him? And what if they were more successful?"

"So maybe Ryan and I were working together on something and had a common enemy?"

"Exactly. I'm going to call Detective Woods." She slid out of the booth and walked outside the restaurant. Through the window, Zane saw her dig her cell phone from the small purse she still wore strapped across her chest. He asked for their check and paid it with the twenty Kinsey had loaned him, before walking outside just as she was severing the connection.

"Did he say anything about me running out on him?" Zane asked.

"He was annoyed, but I don't think he was too surprised. He told me to tell you he heard back from the other three tractor stores, two more in Utah and one in Idaho. Nobody there recognizes you, either. He also showed your picture to the grocer and he confirmed it was you. Anyway, I told Woods about Ryan. They haven't had any murders where the victim fits Ryan's description, but he seemed glad to maybe have another piece of the Zane Doe picture."

"If he can see a picture in all this, he's a better man than I am. Let's get out of here. How far away is Dallas?"

"A couple of hours give or take."

"How do you feel about me driving the car?"

"I feel fine about it. But until we get out of town, why don't I drive? I actually went this way last year when I attended an art show, so I'm familiar with the roads."

"That's fine," he said. "I'd probably get us lost in five minutes."

"Stick with me," she said.

"That's my plan." After paying the tab and leaving a tip, he had about fifty cents to his name and that was only because he hadn't eaten much. It was irritating to have no money. He had a feeling being broke wasn't normal for him. Look at his boots, for instance. They screamed expensive. And there was that comment from Kinsey about the pricey clothes he'd been wearing.

He laughed to himself. For all he knew, he'd spent his last penny on fancy duds to impress some girl or maybe he stole those items or they belonged to this Ryan fellow he was mixed up with.

Who knew?

THAT MOMENT IN the restaurant when she and Zane had stared hard at each other had rattled Kinsey more than she cared to admit. Her funky green car really was on the small side and he was a large guy. She was super aware of him being only a few inches away, and repeatedly cautioned herself to remember he may well be attached to someone else.

It was more difficult to rein in her emotions than it had ever been before. How many times had she found a guy interesting, only to discover she and her mom would be pulling up stakes and starting over? Goodbye followed goodbye until she thought she'd grown numb to them. The result of that was a certain resignation. She could live without love.

Besides, what did love lead to? Marriage. And what was the point of a marriage if not to provide a home for children? Face it, babies required a level of selflessness Kinsey wasn't sure she was up to. In so many ways it seemed to her she'd already raised a child: her mother. She was finally free, why couldn't she just be happy with that?

The answer was sitting next to her. How had everything changed with the arrival of a man without a name or a past or even a safe future? How had he done it? Did she dare grow more attached to him? Wasn't that a perfect blueprint for misery?

These thoughts raced through her head. Though she'd only driven a couple of miles since the restaurant, it seemed as though they'd been back in the car for an hour. She was exhausted. Thank heaven the traffic was easing up and Zane could take over.

"There's a bridge up ahead," she murmured. "I'll pull over after we go under it and you can drive."

"Great," Zane said as he peered through the windshield. "I wonder what that's all about," he added, pointing at the top of the bridge.

Kinsey darted a glance where he gestured. The bridge didn't seem to have any moving traffic. A lone white truck stood out against the rapidly fading light. It was stationary, parked directly above their lane. Leaning on the railing looking down was the indistinct figure of a man.

"God, I hope he's not going to jump," she said as the car neared the bridge.

Suddenly, Zane reached across Kinsey and grasped the wheel, turning the car hard to the right. Kinsey stomped down on the brakes. Overhead, a shower of shrapnel hit the hood and the top of the car before they found the protection of the bridge itself. They hit the sidewalk curb, bounced into a pillar and then back onto the road. Cars whizzed past, honking alarm, apparently unaffected by whatever had fallen. Dead headlamps, ominous popping noises and sluggish steering announced the run-in with the pillar had come with a price. Kinsey yanked hard on the wheel, struggling to control the vehicle, though she could barely see where they were going, thanks to the spiderweb of cracks now crisscrossing the windshield.

"Pull over!" Zane shouted, and once again lent his muscle to hers. They rolled from beneath the bridge, emerging on the other side and to the oasis of a small turnout.

Zane was out of the car in a flash. Kinsey followed suit. She had no idea what had hit them, although it seemed to her that there were too many thumps and crashes to be a single body. And yet, in the corner of her mind, she could see one large oblong object falling toward them before all hell broke loose.

Had that oblong shape been a human being?

Zane took her hand. It was dark under the bridge, though car headlights revealed the broken glass from her little green car. They moved carefully along the sidewalk, dreading what awaited them. Debris in the road showed up as weird shapes they couldn't immediately identify.

"Over there," Zane said, pointing at a long

object sitting on the verge beside the road. Kinsey held her breath as they approached.

She expelled her breath when she saw it wasn't a human being. "It's a box," she said, taking in the long rectangular shape. It appeared to be metal, three feet long, twelve or fourteen inches wide, twisted now, the lid clasps open, the lid itself askew. It didn't look as though it had been there long as the grass beneath and around it showed no signs it had begun to grow up around the sides and no rust had attacked the myriad of dents and scratches.

"A toolbox," Zane said.

"And all that stuff on the road…those are tools," Kinsey added. "That maniac threw a toolbox off the bridge. He could have killed us!"

They both looked up toward the top of the bridge at the same time. It was darker than it had been, but the bridge lights had flickered on. There was no longer a truck—or a man—in sight.

"What are the odds we would be in the car happening to pass under the bridge at that exact moment?" Zane said, lowering his gaze to connect with Kinsey's. She didn't miss the edge of sarcasm in his voice.

They both fell silent as their minds worked overtime, or at least that was Kinsey's excuse for the chill that cut through the humid air. She'd felt this same way just the day before when she'd stood on a New Orleans sidewalk and watched a fake messenger push Zane into a busy street. The sound of approaching sirens, along with the sight of pulsating lights, assured them another driver must have called the police.

"Here we go again," Zane said softly.

Kinsey was just glad he was still holding her hand because her knees felt like cooked noodles. She didn't think the fact that the box hurled toward their car spewing missiles of destruction had anything to do with coincidence.

And she couldn't believe Zane thought so, either.

Chapter Six

"Had to be kids," Sheriff Crown said with a slow shake of his head. "Parents let them run wild nowadays. What starts out as a prank can turn deadly in the blink of an eye."

They'd been driven to the sheriff's office. The deputy who had responded to the call stood in the doorway. "You think it might have been the Owen boys, Sheriff?"

"Could have been," the sheriff said. "Their daddy has a big old white truck. You better drive on out there." An older man with a gray mustache, he appeared to be at the end of his lawmaker career. He sat back in his chair and shook his head again. "You folks were mighty lucky."

"They pretty much killed my car," Kinsey said. Zane had to agree. The police tow truck had hauled it to a garage that wouldn't be open until the next day. Zane suspected Kinsey's insurance would total it outright.

But for now they were stuck. There was no way in the world Zane could pay for any of this, not the car, not a hotel, not even breakfast tomorrow morning, at least not right this minute. And Kinsey was not rolling in money. He marveled at how composed she looked in the midst of this disaster. Maybe, like him, she was counting her lucky stars that the toolbox hadn't landed on her windshield. If it had, he doubted either one of them would be sitting here.

He felt positive the sheriff was on the wrong track thinking this was the act of misguided, rambunctious kids looking for excitement on a Saturday night. Zane would bet his life that the guy on top of that bridge had been waiting for Kinsey's distinctive green car and the passengers it contained. It was the same kind of spontaneous deadly act as the other two attempts, using the means at hand, in this case a toolbox that had probably rattled around in the back of his truck for ages.

Zane knew why he wasn't telling the sheriff about his suspicions. He didn't want to get tied up in statements and red tape. He didn't want to sit in this small burg of a town waiting for the law to figure things out while their assailant had time to plot his next move.

The question got to be why Kinsey was going along with the sheriff's suppositions. Why wasn't she launching into a recital of the events leading up to tonight?

She suddenly stood up. "Sheriff, we've told you everything we know about what happened."

He looked down at the paper on his desk. "Lone man, white truck. You don't know what kind of truck and you didn't see anything about the man you can identify. Is that about right?"

"It all happened so fast," Kinsey said.

"That's not much to go on," the sheriff grumbled. "Course, we do have the toolbox to check, and the tools might produce some prints or something else that ties them to someone around here." He pulled at his mustache and added, "Funny thing about that bridge. It's not used much anymore. Once upon a time it led to the Chemco Company back parking lot, but Chemco got involved in a big lawsuit five, six years ago. When they closed up shop, they boarded up the property, so now the bridge doesn't lead anywhere."

"That's why we didn't see any moving traffic up there," Kinsey said.

"And that's why I figure kids are behind this. I put that in the plural because they tend to run in a pack. You might have missed seeing the others. Anyway, they'd know about the bridge. They probably thought it would be funny. Once they set their plan in motion, they undoubtedly got scared and took off like bats out of hell."

Kinsey nodded as though agreeing. "I wonder if we could leave now. You have my phone number if you need anything else."

"Yeah," he said, and rattled it off as though double-checking he had it right. Then he turned his attention to Zane. "You didn't leave me an address or a phone number."

"He lives with me," Kinsey blurted out. "We're engaged."

"And what about the fact you aren't carrying any identification?" the sheriff asked with a pointed look at Zane's still-bruised neck.

Zane adjusted his collar. "I didn't realize I'd forgotten my wallet until we were hours from home. Seeing as I'm still light-headed from that polo accident I told you about, I didn't plan to drive, so I didn't figure it was a problem."

"Sheriff," Kinsey added, "Albuquerque is still a long way from here. My girlfriend is going to be crazy disappointed if we don't show up for her twenty-sixth birthday party."

"You can't drive your car until they get it fixed," the sheriff pointed out.

"I know that. I left my charge card information for the garage with instructions I'd call to hear the damages and okay the work depending on what my insurance company says. For now, could you tell us where to rent a car?"

"Aren't you kind of rattled after what happened?"

"I'm fine," she said firmly.

The sheriff stared at her a second, then at Zane, who did his best to cover his surprise upon hearing Kinsey planned to rent a car. Maybe she was washing her hands of the whole thing and going home. Part of him hoped that was the case.

And a bigger part didn't.

Finally, the older man slapped the top of his desk and nodded. "Deputy Norton will give you a ride to the rental place. You could head on back to Shreveport for more choices—"

"I'm sure we'll find something here," Kinsey interrupted. She put her hand on Zane's shoulder and added, "Come on, honey, it's time to get back on the road."

Zane got to his feet, stumbling just a hair as he put his weight on his left leg, the injury exacerbated by the sprint back under the bridge. Kinsey gripped his arm and steadied him. They picked up the satchel of Bill Dodge's clothes, Kinsey's bag of art supplies she swore she never left behind, and started toward the door.

"You two take care of yourselves," the sheriff called.

Muttering thanks, they escaped while they could.

WITHIN AN HOUR, they were under way again.

"What bothers me is how he—whoever he is—knew about that bridge," Zane said.

"I know," Kinsey whispered.

"How could that be unless this dude is local?"

"I don't know. Maybe he worked at Chemco sometime."

"So he followed us all the way from New Orleans, waited around while we ate dinner, drove ahead to the bridge and then dumped the back of his truck on us?"

She shrugged. "I guess. Either that or it's those kids the sheriff is so fond of."

"I can't quite buy that."

"Neither can I." She sighed. "But maybe the delay coupled with the different rides in different police cars will throw him off."

He was quiet and she decided not to pursue that line of thought. Zane had hardly been traveling in a straight line since this whole ordeal had begun, and yet, whoever was after him seemed to be one step ahead or behind, depending on your point of view.

"You must be really tired," he said.

"I am. Are you okay to drive?"

"Sure. There are lots of big signs directing me to Dallas. I'll get us there."

"And from there to Amarillo," she said around a yawn as she found a good spot to pull off the road.

While Zane acquainted himself with the car, she took the opportunity to call her mother. It was getting late, but her mom answered on the first ring.

"James brought me home from the hospital a half hour ago," she said. "He wanted to come inside, but he looked so tired. When I went to my room, I found it had been searched."

"By who?" Kinsey asked, but added, "It doesn't matter who. Call the police. Leave the house immediately."

"Don't be silly. It had to be Bill's snoopy nephew. I loaded Bill's shotgun and walked through the whole house. No one is here and I can't see that anything was taken."

Ignoring the image of her tiny mother hauling a shotgun around an old mansion with four floors, if you counted the attic and the basement, Kinsey repeated her warning. "Please, leave for the night. Go to a hotel."

"Nonsense."

Time to give up on that, Kinsey decided. "How is Mr. Dodge?"

"His breathing is better, but we all know it's only a matter of time. He wants to come home. Maybe tomorrow, they said." She paused for a long second and Kinsey imagined her mother's moist eyes. "I'm not sure what I'll do when he dies."

"You always warn me not to look too far ahead," Kinsey said softly.

"Yes, that's true. Listen, why don't you give me a lift to the hospital in the morning and say hi to Bill. He always loves seeing you."

"Well, actually, I can't," Kinsey said.

"The gallery?"

"Not exactly. See, my doctor friend—"

"Wait just a second. That man is no more a doctor than I am. Did you see his hands? Those are not the hands of a professional. What's going on?"

"I didn't intend to mislead you," Kinsey said, which was a half truth at the very best. "Things just kind of got out of hand. You don't need to worry about me."

"I've been worrying about you since the day you were born," her mother said. "I sacrificed just about everything for you."

Kinsey had never heard her mother say anything about sacrificing everything and it jarred her. What did she mean?

"Tell me about this man."

"I just met him yesterday," Kinsey said. "He was in an…accident. He can't remember his name. I'm trying to help him. We're on our way to Utah where he has a kind of a lead."

After everything that had happened, Kinsey didn't think she'd ever gotten around to admitting to her mother that Zane had been asking specifically about her before his injury. She wasn't about to bring it up now, especially since she was still trying to figure out the unspoken antagonistic edge of this conversation. Her mother made leaps of her own, however. "Why was he asking *me* so many questions this morning?" she demanded. "What does that cowboy want with me?"

Kinsey paused before stammering, "Why… why do you call him a…a…cowboy?"

"Those boots," her mother said.

"Lots of ordinary people wear boots, Mom."

"He left here in a Western shirt and jeans wearing those boots and looked totally at home. The way he walked, that swagger! And you heard him talk. Even his tan and his haircut announce who and what he is. That man is a cowboy, Kinsey, no matter what silly story he's feeding you. And you can't trust a cowboy. They're dangerous. They want one thing and one thing only. Please, wherever you are, just come back to New Orleans. Wash your hands of him."

"What do you mean the way he talks? What about it?" Kinsey asked. And since when did her mother lump cowboys into the same group as sex offenders?

"Come home," Frances Frost repeated.

"Not yet."

"Now!"

"I stopped taking orders quite a while ago," Kinsey said softly.

"You're just like your mother!" Frances sputtered.

"I'll take that as a compliment. End of story."

"You said it, not me," her mother snapped and the line went dead.

Kinsey slid into the passenger seat, still dazed by the conversation. When Zane touched her cheek with a gentle caress, she almost jumped out of her skin.

"Hey, are you okay?" he asked. "Is something wrong at home?"

I sacrificed just about everything for you…

"Kinsey? Just tell me. What's wrong? Do you want to go back?"

"No," she said. "Do you?"

"No. But I feel very uncomfortable with you going into debt helping me, and if that's compounded with family problems, you need to pick your priorities."

She nodded. Internally she knew that she had chosen what was right and necessary.

He cupped her chin, leaned across the midconsole and brushed her lips with his. Instant fire reminded Kinsey she might not be thinking totally with her head.

As he started the car, she leaned back and closed her eyes. She'd dealt with a lot of confusion in her life, the by-product of her mother's personality and tumultuous lifestyle. But this took the cake.

KINSEY'S EYES DRIFTED OPEN. The reassuring sounds and motion of the moving car almost lulled her back to sleep, until the bright sunlight bathing her face registered in her brain. She sat up abruptly.

"Morning," Zane said. She looked around. The countryside zooming by was dry, rural, a hundred shades of brown. How had she managed to sleep through the entire night? "What time is it?" she croaked.

"Almost seven." He glanced at her again and added, "Someone needs a cup of coffee."

"You can say that again. Where are we?"

"Just outside of Amarillo, headed to Albuquerque. We'll be in St. George by midnight, even with a couple of stops."

"Maybe we should spend the night in Vegas and finish up tomorrow morning," she said. "Otherwise, we may not be able to walk when we get there."

"You're probably right."

"I can't believe you drove all night," she added as she tried to do something with her hair.

"I was wide-awake and anxious to avoid any more falling objects."

"So, nothing happened?"

"Not a thing. I don't think anyone is following us. We do need fuel, though, so keep your eyes peeled for a gas station."

A moment later, she gestured at a billboard beside the road. "Look. Five miles to the Armadillo Roadhouse, home of Dave's famous flapjacks."

"Do you like flapjacks?" he asked her.

"Doesn't everybody?"

"I'd like them better if I was the one buying them for you," he said.

"We'll find out who you are and then you can hit up your friends and family to repay me," she said breezily. There was no reason for him to obsess about this as there wasn't a thing either one of them could do about it. Her card would stretch a bit further, and then they'd have to think of something else. But that was another catastrophe away.

She looked at her phone to see if she'd received any messages while she slept. Neither her mother nor Ryan had called. She knew her mother's reason was out-and-out stubbornness; it was Ryan's fate that worried her. The confusion of the night before resurfaced.

THEY CLEANED UP in the restaurant bathrooms, ate breakfast and filled the car with gas. Kinsey called the hospital and learned Mr. Dodge was being released later that day. At least that much was going right in the world.

Her next call was to her insurance company, then the repair shop. The last call was followed by a moan.

"What did you learn?" Zane asked as he buttered the pancakes that had just arrived.

Kinsey looked at her small stack, her appetite

gone. "The repair shop gave me a number I'm pretty sure the insurance company will deny. That means they'll total the car and give me what their tables tell them it's worth, which isn't enough to actually replace it. Damn."

Zane shook his head. "I was afraid of that. Well, look on the bright side. Maybe I'm rich."

"My car problems are not your fault," she said, and took a bite. Dave's flapjacks were pretty darn tasty.

"If it was an attempt to kill me, I think that's my fault," he said.

"I don't. Let's not talk about it, okay?"

"Sure."

Back in the car, Kinsey drove while Zane dozed fitfully beside her. Her goal was to clear her mind and just go with the flow. She was no stranger to road trips—that's how she and her mother had moved around for years. But then she'd been a child, relying on an adult's decisions, and now she was an adult and Zane was depending on her to keep all the balls in the air.

Ever mindful that someone could be trailing them or driving ahead, her gaze darted between the rearview mirror and the road. She made her hands remain steady on the wheel as she drove under bridges. The saving grace was that it was light outside.

Worries about killers and having no car began to creep in as mile after mile of desert passed outside the windows. She wished Zane would wake up and talk to her, but he looked reasonably comfortable huddled down in his seat.

Her mother was right—he did look like a cowboy.

As the afternoon wore on, Zane's peaceful slumber seemed to be waning. She saw his hands twitch on his thighs, his lashes flutter against his cheeks. She became truly alarmed when he clutched his throat and cried out. A moment later, his eyes flew open and he looked around as though trying to figure out what was going on. His expression was wild.

"You were having a bad dream," she told him. "Do you remember what it was about?"

He blinked several times. "It's kind of vague," he said, his fingers still at his throat as though the choking had just happened. "There was a giant black tree. That's all I can remember."

"Sounds like something out of a kid's nightmare," she said.

By the time they rolled down Las Vegas's brilliantly lit main street, Kinsey's muscles were knotted from all the sitting. For once, she wasn't hungry—all she wanted to do was move.

They checked into a small motel off the beaten track. The room held a single bed that they both stared at. Kinsey was thinking it was going to be hard to curl up in a bed with Zane mere inches away and get any kind of sleep at all. She didn't know what he was thinking, but by the smoldering look he cast her way, she figured it was along similar lines.

"Maybe we should get out of here for a while," he said.

"Good idea."

The evening was very warm without any of the river breezes that sometimes helped cool things down in New Orleans. They found a casino with a cheap buffet, then followed their ears to a band playing old rock songs from the sixties.

"I need to move around," Kinsey said, looking at the small wooden dance floor.

"I'll give it a try," Zane said.

"Is your left leg up to it?"

"I'll just pretend I'm moving," he said and did just that as Kinsey flexed tight muscles. She loved the familiar beats, singing along with the band when she knew the lyrics and earning a round of applause from a couple of older guys taking a break from keno.

"How do you know the words to these songs?" Zane asked as they came together for a slow dance.

"It's my mom's favorite music," she said close to his ear. It was heaven to be held against his firm chest, to have his warm breath on her neck and cheek, his hand planted on her lower back. She closed her eyes and let the rhythm soothe away the long hours in the car.

"You're very close to her, aren't you?"

Kinsey thought about that for a minute. "Yes and no," she said. "She was the center of my universe because there were so few other constants."

"How about grandparents?"

"My dad was an orphan and Mom's parents died before I was born. I was all she had."

"Well, at least she had you."

"Yeah. But that's a big load for a kid to carry, you know, to be everything. It's harder than it sounds."

"I bet it is," he said, looking down into her eyes, and they both smiled. "I wonder what my childhood was like," he added.

"You'll reclaim your memories," she said softly, her gaze on his mouth and the perfect shape of his lips. She'd tasted them several times now, but that didn't mean she didn't want to sample them again.

"And if I don't, I'll have you," he said, and she wasn't sure if he meant in the figurative sense of memories of her or actually having her—at his side, in his bed, sharing his life.

Once again she cautioned herself to slow down. Zane was an enigma and would be until he found his place in the world and remembered why he was in New Orleans, why he'd asked about her mother, what he knew about Ryan.

Soon enough, it was time to return to the

motel. They took a cab in the hopes that if they had a tail, it might throw them off. Once back in the room with the dead bolt in place and curtains drawn, they took turns using the shower. Zane had some of Bill Dodge's garments to change into and Kinsey had grabbed a long beach cover-up off a sale rack in the casino basement. It was a weird shade of orange, which probably explained its cheap price tag, but at least it was clean. By the time she was ready for bed, Zane had already chosen a side. She took the other. She was nervous and excited and full of cautionary tales that ran through her head like the ticker tape she'd once seen in an old movie.

"It feels great to lie down," Zane said as his hand found hers and clasped it.

"I wish I knew if you were married," Kinsey said and then wished she hadn't. Why couldn't she just shut up and scoot over to her side of the bed and go to sleep?

"I do, too." He turned on his side, facing her. Their faces were close, their hands joined. Every inch of Kinsey's body ached with awareness and desire, and by the tone of Zane's breathing, she knew he was in similar distress.

"I can't believe I've ever felt this way about anyone else," he said, his fingers caressing her arms.

"I know I haven't," she said. "You're making me want things I never wanted before."

"Like what?"

"A future with one person."

"And children?"

"I don't know."

"I like kids," he said.

"Why?" she asked.

"The usual things. Their innocence, their trust. What they represent when it comes to playing life forward. On a gut level I guess I feel they're what matters, they're the point of it all." He paused. "Why are you uncertain?"

Kinsey's mother's comment about sacrificing everything rang once again in her mind. Now she wondered why it came as such a surprise. Was it because Kinsey had always felt as if she was the one called upon to make concessions, helpless to lead a normal life because of her mother's idiosyncrasies? "I guess in a way I feel like I've already raised a child," she murmured. "My mother."

"Nurturing a brand-new baby would be way different than dealing with a grown-up," he said.

"I would hope so," she responded with a chuckle, but it died in her throat as his lips touched her cheek.

"I want to kiss you," he murmured against her skin.

"You just did," she answered softly.

"Not like that," he said, moving closer still, his arm sliding under her shoulders, pulling her against him. He licked her earlobe, nuzzled her throat, showered a dozen moist kisses on her neck, on her shoulder, across her clavicle. Her breasts throbbed with a wanton pulse that drummed inside her body like a jungle beat. By the time his lips touched hers, she was half gone, and she returned his kiss with the pent-up longing of every moment she'd been aware of his existence.

She wanted his gentle, warm hands to touch every inch of her and she could tell by the erection pressing against her thigh that his longings equaled her own. It felt like destiny. The ticker-tape machine fell silent, warnings ceased; she was his for the taking. Even the fact that this zero-to-ninety reaction had happened in mere moments and with a man who remained a virtual stranger failed to rouse her consciousness.

And then he paused as though similar thoughts had detonated in his brain. The slight hesitation was enough to reawaken Kinsey's common sense.

If they kept racing down this particular mountain, they would end up having sex, right here, tonight. And tomorrow when he rediscovered a wife? They would have to live with this act, with this decision.

The sex-hungry part of her brain whispered: *you would have this night to remember. Isn't that enough?*

He rolled over on his back and swore. A sigh passed his lips next, and then his cheek grazed her shoulder.

She sat up abruptly, unable to bear his touch, though she hungered for it with every ounce of her being. His hand landed on her back and she flinched. "I'm sorry," he whispered. The bed creaked as he sat up behind her. His arms circled her and he spoke against her hair. "This is my fault."

She didn't even try to respond.

"You're right about me," he continued, "about not knowing what obligations and responsibilities I already have in my life. I shouldn't have started this, it was weak to give in to the lust I feel for you when I have absolutely nothing to offer, not even tomorrow."

"I didn't exactly try to stop you," Kinsey said softly.

His lips touched her shoulder. "Stick with me for another day, Kinsey, and forgive me for putting you in this position."

She turned her head a little and closed her eyes. She was as much at fault as he. She nodded and he hugged her. When he lay back down, he pulled her with him and she tried to relax by his side.

She'd known better than to let herself get mixed up with him at this stage of his quest. She'd ignored her common sense. She wouldn't do that again.

Chapter Seven

They set out early, but the night before had been
restless and uneasy. It took two hours to drive to
St. George. Nestled in a valley and surrounded
by red cliffs, it was larger than Zane had expected and very pretty with its green trees and
steepled white buildings.

"Getting nervous?" she asked. She'd been po-
lite but reserved during the whole drive, a par-
ody of her former warmth. Last night had been
hard on both of them.

"A little," he said. "I could walk into a tractor dealership in a few moments and someone
could call me by name."

Kinsey nodded toward her small handbag on
the console between them. "Dig out my phone
and look up Travers's Tractors so we don't get
lost."

"Sure." He opened the clasp, but there was
a book stuffed inside the bag, making a search
tricky.

"I'm sorry," she said after glancing at him.

"It's not in there. It should be in one of the pockets on the outside."

"What book is this?" he asked.

She glanced at him. "It's an art book Bill Dodge gave me because it concerns women artists. I think he must have rebound it himself. I wanted to ask him, but things got out of hand and I didn't get a chance."

"What I can see of it is very pretty." He closed the main bag and discovered the phone where she'd said he would. He found it oddly comforting that he knew how to use the device. So why didn't he know anything about himself and the people he loved?

He glanced at Kinsey. *Please, let there be no one else,* he said inside his head. His biggest fear was that he'd find a wife and children waiting for him and he would not remember them. He'd have to stay with them, but his heart would beat for Kinsey. She would go back to her life, and he would have to find a way to come to grips with his.

He directed Kinsey through the quiet streets to the other side of town. For some reason Zane couldn't explain, neither one of them seemed worried today about an assailant. He noticed Kinsey rarely checked her mirrors and his heart hadn't skipped a beat every time they drove beneath an overpass.

"There it is," he said, looking ahead at the

green sign with the words *Travers's Tractors and Farm Equipment* written in white. His throat felt dry and he turned up his collar although the bruises had grown dark now and hiding them was nearly impossible.

Kinsey pulled into a large parking lot that held a few trucks.

"Let's get this over with," he said, opening his door.

The store consisted of a big showroom filled with tractors and attachments. The only other people were a salesman showing an elderly couple a mower, and another salesman who approached them with a huge smile. "Howdy, folks," he said, putting out a hand. "My name is Ted Baxter. You looking for a tractor?" As they shook hands, Ted frowned and then nodded. "I've seen you before," he said.

Zane's pulse quickened and he felt Kinsey's body tense. "You have?"

"Sure. I remember now. The police faxed us your photo. Am I right? That's you, isn't it?"

Hope that he'd be recognized by the first person he met flared and died within a few short sentences. "That's me," he said. "I hoped that walking in here might trigger someone's memory."

"I'm real sorry for your predicament."

The elderly couple walked past them toward the door, deep in conversation. Their salesman drifted over to Ted's side and stared at Zane in a way that suggested he, too, recognized him from a photo.

"Can you tell us where your other franchises are located?" Kinsey asked.

"Sure. Heck, I've got a brochure in my office."

Zane had taken the key fob out of his pocket and showed it now to the two men. "Before you get that brochure, do either of you recognize this?"

"Red Hot," Ted said as he turned it over in his hand. "That's a small tractor made by Bolo, kind of the sporty model. There, in the corner, that's what they look like. But I've never seen a key ring—"

"I have," the other salesman said. "About four or five years ago. They ran a promotion when the model first came out. We had these little disks printed for all the stores. Someone made a mistake and this branch's address ended up on every one of them. Manufacturer cut us a deal, so we used them anyway."

"All the stores?"

"Yeah. Most of them just made up little fake keys with their own branch's location. Those never lasted long."

"So you don't know which store this came from?" Kinsey persisted.

"No. Sorry."

Ted ran off to get the brochure. Back in seconds, he turned the pamphlet over where five franchises were listed. "It had to come from one of these," Ted said.

The other salesman looked at the list. "Wait a second. How about the Falls Bluff branch?"

"What Falls Bluff branch?" Ted asked.

"Falls Bluff, Idaho. Wait. I forgot—you weren't here four years ago. Right after the Red Hot promotion began, the branch in Falls Bluff closed its doors. I heard that someone bought the property and opened their own farm equipment business. Some of the same people might still work there, though."

"Do you know the name of the new place?" Zane asked.

"No, sorry, I don't. It was on Festival Street, though. I doubt you'll miss it."

Five minutes later, they were headed north on their way to Bryce Canyon where they would find the next Travers's Tractors, and from there to Salt Lake City, then into Idaho—Twin Falls first, then Falls Bluff, final destination Coeur d'Alene.

BY THAT NIGHT, they were both travel weary. Utah had been a bust and they'd forced themselves to keep going until they got to the Idaho border. Since it was way too late to worry about things like debt, Kinsey bought them both clean clothes at a department store just minutes after hearing her car had been totaled. She would receive well under a thousand dollars for the little lime bug and it rankled.

Tomorrow they would go to three more stores, but Kinsey had kind of given up hope and she could tell that Zane had, too. They were weary of sitting, asking the same questions in almost identical venues, looking over their shoulders and eating fast food.

There'd been no sign that day that anyone was interested in them, and Kinsey began to think that maybe Sheriff Crown had been right about the bored kids.

She asked for and received a room with two double beds and locked the dead bolt. She sat cross-legged on her bed for an hour and sketched from memory the woman who had waited on them, an angelic-looking teenager with the unexpected tattoo of barbed wire and tiny red hearts encircling her neck. Even conquering that didn't lighten her mood and she finally lay back on the pillow.

All the while she'd been drawing, she'd been glancing over at Zane lounging atop the other bed clad only in boxers and a T-shirt. He'd borrowed a newspaper from the office, stretched out on his stomach and started the crossword puzzle. Memories of his strength and gentleness tugged at every part of her body.

He seemed to sense her attention and looked

up at her. All the protective layers she'd erected that day teetered under the blue intensity of his gaze. After a second, he crossed the short distance to her side in one step. He had long, straight legs, not quite as tan as his muscular arms and commanding face. He sat on the edge of her mattress.

For several seconds they stared at each other. Kinsey felt as if she was going to explode.

"You look beautiful tonight," he said as he ran a lock of her hair through his fingers. "Of course, you always look beautiful."

"For all the good it does us," she whispered. When he leaned over her and kissed her cheek, she turned her face. "Don't," she whispered.

"Sorry," he said, and slowly sat up. He didn't leave, however, just sat there, still and silent, one hand on her shoulder as he stared around the room. Finally he looked down at her again. "Last night I asked you to give me one more day. That day is now over. I think you should drive away tomorrow and let me finish this."

"You keep forgetting about my mother," she said. "You were asking questions about her. I need to know why so I can protect her."

"It's more than that," he protested. "Whoever took my wallet knows where I live. He might have swiped a cell phone, too, which would reveal even more about me. We have to stay alert and be prepared for the worst if we actually find out where I'm from."

"You're talking about another ambush?"

"He could be there before us."

"I'm staying with you until Coeur d'Alene," she said. "I have a feeling about that place. Let's get some sleep, okay?"

Before he got back in bed, he snatched the chair at the desk and levered it under the knob.

In the morning she called her mother and found out Bill was home and the dreaded nephew had shown up full of demands. "He treats this place like it's his already," Frances fumed. "Always prowling around, looking for something. And he grew a beard. All that red hair—he looks like a Viking. Anyway, where are you now?"

"Idaho. Just a couple of places to check."

Frances was silent for several beats before she said, "Idaho?"

"Yeah," Kinsey said. "One of the few states we didn't live in."

"We were there for a few months when you were three. You just don't remember. I have to go. Chad is taking apart Bill's desk." The phone clicked off.

Zane had come into the room. "Your mother?" he said.

"How did you know?"

"You get a certain look in your eyes after you talk to her." Kinsey actually cracked a smile.

The Twin Falls Travers's Tractors was a bust, just like the others. They reached Falls Bluff by noon, their expectations rock bottom. The town's namesake seemed to be the flat-faced mountain that sported a waterfall located to the north. Evergreens covered the hillsides surrounding the town, while open plains baked in the sun.

The city was tiny and Festival Street was easy to find. So was the green-and-white sign repainted with the name Shorty's. The interior didn't resemble a Travers's outlet. There were no cubicles, no open floor space. Every inch seemed to be crammed with shelves displaying must-have country equipment and goods.

There was no one in sight, so they bided their time, unsure how to attract attention, listening to a country-western station on the radio. Finally, they heard a noise coming from the back and turned in time to see a young woman enter the room carrying a forty-pound sack of feed. She dropped it next to the counter and slapped her hands together. Strawberry-blond pigtails on either side of her head made her look younger than a probable age of twenty. Looking right at Zane, she called, "Hey, Gerard, I didn't know anyone was out here. Hope you haven't been waiting long."

The song on the radio seemed to fade away as a moment in time stretched endlessly inside

Kinsey's head. This girl knew Zane. Was this it? His name was Gerard?

"Just in town, thought I'd stop by," Zane said. It appeared he wasn't going to announce amnesia if he didn't have to.

"He's showing me around," Kinsey added. "I'm visiting from New Orleans." The girl didn't respond to New Orleans, so apparently it wasn't a place she associated with Gerard.

"Long as you're here, do you want to pick up Pike's order?" She rounded the counter and opened a box, riffled through receipts and read aloud. "Galvanized fencing staples, half a dozen sacks of oats and molasses horse feed, dog food and two reels of utility chain. Oh, and he wants a dozen calf bottles." She looked up at Zane and added, "I have most of the order put together out back. You can pull your truck around to the loading doors."

"I don't have the truck with me," he said and Kinsey could see he was angling his head to get a look at the order. The salesgirl noticed him doing this and handed it over. Kinsey looked, as well.

The order was made by someone named Pike Hastings and was billed to the Hastings Ridge Ranch, Falls Bluff, Idaho.

How was Zane, or rather, Gerard, related to Pike Hastings?

The girl must have been a mind reader. "Tell

your brother everything is here whenever he wants to come into town and get it."

"I will," Zane said, his voice kind of hollow.

The girl turned her attention to Kinsey. "Did you know Lily from before she got married?"

Lily? Was this a sister or was this a wife? More to the point, was this Zane's wife? Kinsey bit her lip and tried not to look as shaken as she felt. She murmured, "No, I didn't."

The mention of a woman and the word *married* in the same sentence seemed to affect Zane in the same way it had her. He quietly handed the order form back to the girl, who plopped it in the box. Kinsey could feel the tension coursing through his body and she suspected he needed to get out of that store and decompress. She knew she did. "It's about time we get back," she said vaguely, waving in the direction of the door.

Zane seemed to suddenly recall the key fob that had played such a big part in this ritual, and he took it from his pocket. "Do you have any more of these?" he asked, showing the girl the Red Hot tag.

She shook her head. "I've never seen one of these before."

"I must have picked it up somewhere else," he said. "Well, see you later."

"Give Lily and Charlie my best."

"Sure thing," Zane said.

PIKE, LILY AND CHARLIE. Three names he should recognize, three people, one of them his brother. Who was Charlie? And Lord, was Lily his wife? Was Charlie his son or father or another brother?

For a minute or two, they both sat side by side in the cocoon of the rental car. Zane finally cleared his throat. "That girl seemed very sure I was Gerard Hastings."

Kinsey looked over at him. Her tongue flicked across her luscious candy-apple lips, her huge eyes glittered like dark water trapped in a cool well. "She did. You are."

"But that doesn't mean Lily is my wife. She didn't actually say that."

"No, she didn't. But you know what, Zane—I mean, Gerard. Wow, that's going to take some getting used to."

"Tell me about it."

"What I was going to say is that for your sake, I hope one look at her and you'll remember who you are and what's important to you. You'll remember who you love."

"I think I know who I love," he whispered with a quick glance into her eyes.

"Don't say that. Listen, all we can do is find out." She took her cell phone from its pocket and brought up the map. Two minutes later, she said, "Here it is. Hastings Ridge Ranch, Route 109." She plugged her phone into the car charger and added, "Twenty miles from here lies what is apparently your home. You'll finally learn the truth."

He stared at her until she lowered her gaze, stuck the keys in the ignition and started the car.

The truth. Would he be able to live with it once he found it?

Chapter Eight

The countryside flattened out as they drove east of town. Zane—he simply could not think of himself as Gerard yet—studied each house, farm and ranch as they sped by. How many hundreds of times he must have traveled this road and yet nothing looked familiar. When they pulled around a yellow school bus, kids waved through the windows. Had he ridden that bus or one like it to school? How far did his past go back here?

The thought that the man who had attacked him might be waiting at the ranch added another level of tension. Even when there ceased being people or houses and the scenery turned into bucolic vistas, his stomach stayed tied in a knot. Kinsey seemed as distracted as he was, which he supposed meant she was just as nervous.

Had he left this place in a huff? Would his family welcome him back or be shocked he'd returned? He didn't know if he'd been away a week or a month. The girl at the store hadn't seemed surprised to see him, so probably not that long. She also hadn't reacted to the mention of New Orleans. Had his destination been a secret and, if so, why?

"It shouldn't be far now," Kinsey said. "It sure seems to be out in the middle of nowhere, doesn't it?"

"Yes," he said uneasily. Did this mean it was a poor ranch struggling to make ends meet? How was he ever going to pay Kinsey back in a timely manner if that was the case?

At the top of the next hill they looked down into a valley of sorts. No buildings were visible from the highway, but they did see a long road accented with a line of power poles bisecting the floor leading to another hill a mile or so away. A small red car drove toward them along that road, a cloud of dust in its wake.

Kinsey stopped the rental at the point where the paved and the gravel road intersected. A herd of cattle, these with calves by their sides, looked up at them, mooed their disapproval and moseyed away from the fence.

"Are you ready for this, Gerard?" Kinsey asked, gesturing at the approaching car.

"Not Gerard, not between us, anyway, not until it means something. And I'm about as ready as I'll ever be. Let's get out and ask the driver if we're at the right place." He stepped from the air-conditioned comfort of the sedan into the summer heat of the day. The smell of animals and dried grass filled the air. A minute later, the red car pulled alongside their rental and the door opened.

A small dynamo of a woman wearing jeans and a T-shirt waved when she saw them. While her expressive dark brows framed equally dark eyes, her hair was very blond and spiky short. Beaded earrings dangled toward her shoulders. "Gerard, I didn't know you were back," she said. "Have you seen your brothers yet?"

Just like that, he learned he had more than one brother. "I…I just got back," he said. Was this Lily?

"What happened to your throat?" she gasped. "And your cheek. Were you in a fight? I thought that was Chance's area of expertise."

It was hard to miss the derogatory tone in her voice. Who was Chance? And who, exactly, was this woman?

"No, not a fight," he said. "I had an accident."

She studied the marks a moment and narrowed her eyes. "That must have been quite the *accident*. It looks to me like someone tried to choke you."

Zane wasn't sure what to say that wouldn't reveal his memory loss and he didn't want to do that right now. Kinsey must have sensed his feelings for she jumped into the silence. "My name is Kinsey Frost," she said, extending her hand.

"Lily Kirk," the woman said and shook Kinsey's hand. "Are you a friend of Gerard's?"

"Yes," Kinsey said.

"I see by your license plate you're from Louisiana."

"The car is a rental," Kinsey said without volunteering any additional information.

Zane, who'd been fooling with his shirt collar, added, "Kinsey and I met a few days ago. She gave me a ride home."

"Where's your truck?"

"I'm not sure," he said.

"That makes no sense." She shook her head. "Never mind, it's none of my business." She glanced at her watch, then peered down the road. "The bus is late. Poor Charlie is stuck on that thing for forty-five minutes coming and going to summer school. It's only for three weeks and heaven knows he needs to be around other kids, but I still feel sorry for the little guy."

She wore a ring on her left hand, but it was hard to tell if it was a wedding band or something else. Zane wondered if she was married to one of his brothers. The last name was wrong, but many women didn't automatically change their name upon marrying.

"We passed a bus about ten miles back," Kinsey said.

"Good, then it'll be here any minute. The gal

who drives that bus knows these roads like the back of her hand."

There was no way to ask the next question that wouldn't be abrupt, so Zane just put it out there. "Is there anyone new at the ranch, say, within the last two days?"

"One guy."

"When did he get here?" Zane asked.

Her eyebrows knit together as she thought. "Not long. What's today, Tuesday? Maybe since Sunday. I guess he asked around town and found out who was hiring. Pike's the only one who talked to him that I know of. He said the guy is a drifter on his way to New Mexico and needed a few weeks' work because he ran out of money. That's all I know. Why?"

"I was just wondering," he said. He glanced at Kinsey and read what she was thinking in her eyes: the timing was pretty darn suspicious. Was this man there for them? Striving to sound casual, he added, "What's he look like?"

"I don't know. I've never met him. Oh, wait. Pike says he has a red beard and I think he said he was about thirty." Kinsey looked startled by the description. Meanwhile, Lily tilted her head as though a thought had just occurred to her. "Where did you run off to, Gerard? No one here knew. Chance just said that you left right after the wedding but wouldn't tell him where you were going or how long you'd be gone. Of course, he could be lying through his teeth and who would guess?"

Zane didn't have the slightest idea what Lily was talking about, but there was the name Chance again and said with the same derision. He tried to look confident as he said, "I'm not trying to be secretive. I'd just like to explain it later, okay?"

She lowered her gaze for a second, then looked back. "I'm sorry I said that about your brother. Sometimes I forget my place."

Grumbling engine noises preceded the arrival of the school bus. It ground to a halt beside them and as Lily walked toward the door, a small boy with fair hair and freckles appeared on the stairs. He was a slightly built kid who wore torn pants and a red-and-white-striped shirt. He jumped off the bus as though exiting a burning building.

"See you tomorrow, Sue," Lily called as she waved the bus off. She looked down at the child and shook her head. "Oh, Charlie, those are your new jeans! How did you get a hole in them already?"

"I don't know," Charlie mumbled.

"Come on, fess up. What happened?"

"Nothin'."

"Charlie, did someone push you again?"

"No," the boy said quickly.

Lily put her hands on her hips. "It was Trevor, wasn't it? I'm going to call his mother."

"Mommy, no!" Charlie said in a panic. "No! Everyone calls me a baby." Suddenly the boy seemed to realize they weren't alone. He looked from Kinsey to Zane and the threatening flood of tears vanished. "You're back!" the child cried.

"Yeah," Zane said. "I'm back."

"I'D LOVE TO paint that woman," Kinsey said as she followed Lily's car down the gravel road. Zane figured Kinsey kept a good distance between them in case Lily's tire threw up a rock. He knew she was nervous about the rental. "She's really pretty, but it's not that. There's something haunting behind her eyes. Did you notice it?"

"No," Zane said truthfully. It was impossible not to recognize Lily's charm and quirkiness, beauty even, but he hadn't looked closely at her, not really. "Her hair is sure blond."

"Bleach," Kinsey said. "It's a good look for her. Different."

"Yeah," he said. Right now, he was just anxious to get to the end of this road and find out what came next. He didn't know if the land they were passing was part of the Hastings ranch or if the ranch existed down one of the smaller roads they'd passed.

Fenced pastures lined either side of the road, the land beyond glowed golden in the afternoon sun, changing from rolling mountains dotted with bright green trees to the high mountains beyond with their permanent cover of evergreens. Every once in a while they would top a rise and catch a glimpse of a river twining its way far below. Cattle grazed everywhere.

They also caught glimpses of houses, some old-fashioned and some very modern, all far off the road and secluded from one another. Each had an assortment of outbuildings and barns.

"Do you remember any of this?" Kinsey asked.

Zane stared out at the rows of mown hay that lay drying in the sun before the hay baler came along and did its work. He didn't know how he knew this, he just did. "Not really. It all seems vaguely familiar. You know, I really don't think Lily and I are married to each other. And she didn't ask if my wife knew I was home. I can't tell you how relieved I am."

"You two could be in the middle of a terrible marriage, I guess, but she didn't treat you that way."

"No, she seemed more or less indifferent to me." He took a deep breath and touched her leg. "There's only one woman in the world I want to be attached to, Kinsey. You know that, right?"

She cast him a serious look. "I know that's what you think now. I know that we're immensely attracted to each other and that if you're single, I can guess what we're going to do about that attraction. But I also know your life right now is one-dimensional. For all intents and purposes, you're four or five days old and I am the single familiar face in a sea of strangers. That could change."

"And you don't want a broken heart," he stated flatly.

"No, do you?"

"No." Though he suspected that one or both of them were going to end up with just that.

They were silent a few seconds and then Kinsey added, "Why didn't you just tell Lily the truth and ask for her help?"

"I don't know for sure," he said.

"I got the impression she's no one's dummy," Kinsey added.

"So did I. I guess I just want to tell my family all at once. There's so much I need to explain, and so much I need explained to me. Lily mentioned a wedding and a guy named Chance and don't forget the new wrangler, which makes me remember you acted kind of weird when she described him."

"That's because she used the same words my mother did to describe Chad Dodge. But it can't be him. I talked to my mother this morning and she was yelling at him. I swear, so much has happened since this morning, it seems like three days have passed."

Zane rubbed his forehead. They grew quiet as they drove by a crew mowing the tall fields of hay, four combines working in harmony across a huge sweep of land. Were any of them family members? While he studied their far-off action, Kinsey crested yet another hill. Her intake of breath earned his attention.

"Holy cow," she said.

The river they'd glimpsed all along made a turn in the valley below them. The acreage on the peninsula that the U-shaped bend created looked green and fertile, with fields rolling to the bank and a road extending down to the river. A big old wooden house sat in a protected alcove. It appeared to be surrounded with concrete and rock decks, most of them covered to provide relief from sun or snow. All the work buildings sat off a distance. Some of them looked very old while others gleamed with new paint. Sunlight glinted off the meandering blue water.

"If that's the Hastings ranch, your chances I can actually repay you for everything you've done just went up," Zane said.

"It's beautiful here," she whispered.

"Beautiful enough to make a portrait artist stick around and try painting a landscape?"

She spared him a brief glance. "We'll see," she said.

KINSEY PULLED UP behind Lily's car, which was parked next to a vibrant fenced garden bursting with squash, beans and corn. The air smelled of herbs. The sound of running water echoed across the land while the drone of insects and the distant braying of cattle added other dimensions. All and all, it smelled, felt and tasted like summer.

They were immediately beset upon by a trio of dogs who woofed and wagged their greetings nonstop. Two seemed to be shepherds with black-and-white fur, perky ears and mischievous eyes. The third looked like a Lab mix, kind of a rusty brown. All of them paid their respects to Kinsey but focused most of their canine love on Zane.

He knelt and petted each in turn, suffered the occasional tongue washing with a smile and ruffled soft ears all around.

"They like you," Kinsey said.

"Who doesn't love a dog?" he replied. He looked up at her with eyes bluer than the vast sky above and added, "Did you have a dog when you were a kid?"

"No," she said. How did you have a dog when you never owned a house? Not many of the rentals her mother could afford allowed pets and Kinsey had been denied as much as a goldfish.

Zane straightened and they both surveyed the house. Up close it remained the sprawling log structure they'd seen from above, but it loomed even bigger.

"I have work to do," Lily called as she ushered

Charlie up a short flight of stone steps to a small deck complete with a narrow wooden bench. The child yanked open the door and scooted inside the house, but Lily paused before following her son. "Are you guys eating with us tonight or are you going back to your house?"

The question seemed to stump him. He looked at Kinsey, who wasn't sure what to say, then back at Lily. "Thanks, we'll eat here if you have enough."

"Are you coming in now?"

"Uh, no. I want to look around."

"Gotta say hi to Rose, I bet."

"Yes, where is she, do you know?"

"The barn," Lily said. "Where else would she be? Honestly, Gerard."

He squared his shoulders. "Where is everyone…else?"

Her brow furled as if confused. "Your dad is on his honeymoon and your brothers are out in the east field doing a health inspection on a group of heifers. There's no one else here except me and Charlie."

"What about the new ranch hand? Where is he?"

"Probably out with the mowing crew. How would I know? Chance doesn't exactly discuss work details with me, you know. I'm just the hired help."

"Will there be a chance for me to talk to my brothers before dinner?"

Lily hitched her hands on her waist and narrowed her eyes. "I know I'm too mouthy for my own good, but wow, you're sure acting strange. In about three hours, just like always, whoever is here will collapse in the library to look through the mail. You usually join them, lately, anyway, well, since…" Her voice tapered off, she glanced at Kinsey, then away. A second later she turned and walked into the house.

"I wonder what that was all about," Zane said.

Kinsey shrugged.

"She apparently works here," Zane said. "She's obviously not my wife. And apparently, I don't live at this house."

"Yes," Kinsey said and wondered if it meant anything that Lily hadn't mentioned a wife at home waiting for him. It was impossible to know without asking and it was clear Zane wasn't going to ask until he saw his brothers.

He shook his head. "It's all too much. No way do I want to go inside and make small talk for three hours. Let's go find the barn."

"What about the possibility of an ambush?"

"We'll keep our eyes open."

"Okay, I'm with you."

The dogs frolicked around their legs as they headed toward the most obvious building. It turned out to be relatively new and set up for horses. There was no one about—even the stalls were empty except one. Within this space resided a swaybacked mare with a graying red mane. The horse looked as if she was getting on in years, and though the outside door of her stall stood open, she contentedly munched hay from a holder. A sign over her stall read Rose and looked as though it had been made a long time ago with a wood-burning kit.

"I don't think she's going to have a lot to tell us," Zane said as the mare ambled up to him. He reached out to touch her and she closed her big brown eyes. Kinsey got the profound feeling that the horse recognized Zane and that there was affection between them. Or would be when Zane finally remembered his past and became Gerard again.

As she took out her phone, Zane ran his head down the old mare's face. "You're a sweet thing, aren't you?" he said gently. She nuzzled his neck and made a deep grumbling sound in her throat. After a few minutes, they exited through the door on the other end of the barn and found a shaded pasture with a dozen horses grazing on grass. "Who are you calling?" Zane asked as Kinsey once again attempted a call.

"Detective Woods. There's no reception, though."

"Why Woods?"

"Don't you think he should know your identity? It will change the way he conducts his investigation."

"If we wait until tomorrow, I might have actual details to share," he pointed out. "Like maybe the license number of my truck or travel dates he can check. Maybe one of my brothers knew my plans. Lily intimated that Chance doesn't always tell everything he knows."

Several glistening animals had looked up at them and one, a lovely black gelding, trotted to the fence, his mane and tail flying out behind him. The horse came to a stop opposite Zane. Snorting, he stretched his head over the top railing and bumped Zane's shoulder with his velvety nose. Zane laughed as he leaned against the fence, the horse's big black head right beside his own. They were joined a moment later by a smaller horse, dappled gray, with a delicate head and huge liquid eyes. She sniffed Kinsey's hair.

Zane laughed again. Honestly, he might not remember being Gerard Hastings, but it was as if he'd started to come back to life the minute his feet hit Hastings's earth. "You know, I have to assume these horses are mine to ride whenever I want," he said. "I know you're not really dressed for it, but do you know how to ride a horse, Kinsey?"

"Kind of. It's been a few years, but maybe it's like a bike, maybe you don't forget."

"That's what I'm banking on. Let's saddle up

these two and take off toward the ridge behind the house. It beats finding someplace to hide until eight o'clock tonight. And if that new wrangler gets word we're here, I'd just as soon be a little harder to find."

Kinsey looked down at the white pants she'd washed out in the sink the night before, and the black shirt she'd bought the day before that. The sandals weren't great for riding, but she should be okay if the horse didn't step on her. "After you," she said with a sweeping gesture of her arm.

THEY FOUND ALL the equipment easily, as the barn was a model of organization. Though the dogs settled in to watch the saddling process, they didn't follow when Zane and Kinsey led the rides from the barn.

Knowing the horse had a far better chance of finding the right trails, Zane provided gentle pressure to go in a general direction but left most of the decisions to the animal. In that way, they entered a wooded area where the air was noticeably cooler. They soon came across a small tributary stream that fed to the river. Once they'd waded across, the land began to rise. Eventually, the woods thinned out.

Zane felt no sense of fear out here. He began to rethink the whole bridge incident. Had they jumped to a false conclusion? Had there been just too much going on to think clearly or was his thinking slow because of his compromised physical condition?

One thing that wasn't slow was his heartbeat when he turned in the saddle and looked back at Kinsey riding the little Arabian mare. When she looked up and met his gaze, her ruby lips curved. Now that he was home, even if it turned out he wasn't attached to another woman, would she go back to New Orleans and her mother and her job and her life? She had to have friends and connections in Louisiana, while she had none here. Why would she stay? To get to know him? To be with him, to be his lover? Would that be enough for her?

The trees continued thinning as the land stopped climbing, and now they could see through the branches to a broad field dotted with the huge umbrella shapes of oak trees. This was the top of the ridge, he figured, and more than anything he'd seen yet, it struck a chord with him.

Something drew him west and he went with his gut. The horse was a smooth ride, full of energy and strong. He could hear the hooves of Kinsey's steed behind him and glanced over his shoulder to make sure she was still in the saddle. Not only was she there, she was smiling, apparently enjoying herself as much as he was.

Within a few hundred feet, an odd sense of

familiarity slowly turned to one of dread. A minute later, gut clenching, he realized what it was.

The dream he'd had in the hospital: *the rolling gold grass, the chase, the looming tree with the gnarled claws as roots*. The choking, gasping…

Here it was, the tree, not bare and black, but leafy and vibrant and yet menacing. Branches thick as rum barrels ran parallel to the ground like suspended bridges, more animal than plant. The towering tree made his skin crawl and he didn't know why. The horse had come to a halt and now he slid out of the saddle, boots hitting the ground, careful not to stand in the shade it cast, uneasy and nervous.

Was someone else here? Was this response really to a tree or to the sense they were being watched, followed? He turned suddenly. Where was Kinsey?

Right behind him. He'd lost track of her for a few moments, hadn't noticed the sound of her horse approaching or felt her presence as she dismounted.

"What's wrong?" she asked. Her dark eyes reflected his confusion.

He shook his head as he allowed his gaze to take in a 360-degree view. There was no one else around and very few hiding spots. "Nothing." How could he tell her he'd been spooked by a tree? "Let's see what's over there," he added, and pointed farther west, willing to go almost anywhere as long as it took him away from here. He climbed back on the black horse, waited for Kinsey to mount the Arabian, and together they took off toward the distant mountains.

Within a couple of miles, his breathing returned to normal and he began to question the reaction that had taken him by surprise. The land once again changed character, and evidence of human occupation started to appear. At first it was the fact the trails turned into roads with rutted grooves that wagon wheels must have dug in the past. Then it was old wooden fences rotting on their rock-pile posts, abandoned roads leading into the distance and signs that a railroad had once existed although the tracks were now overgrown. They reined in the horses when they saw several structures up ahead and heard the sound of a river. Crossing a rickety bridge, they found themselves in a cluster of buildings lining either side of a street.

"It's an old ghost town," Kinsey murmured as they slowly rode between the decrepit wooden structures. Here and there a bit of paint remained, the BAN of a bank, for instance. Cracked glass in the dark windows and decaying wooden sidewalks were decorated with what appeared to be new no-trespassing signs. They rode silently to the end of the town and stopped before reaching an array of rusting mining equipment.

Kinsey cleared her throat and he looked at

her. Her fine dark hair had come loose from her ponytail and swept across her forehead and cheeks. Her lips, as always, resembled heart-shaped candies, her eyes burned with curiosity and her skin had attained a slight blush from the sun. For a second, he thought of what he knew of her childhood and what he'd seen and heard of her mother and he wondered how she'd managed to come out of it so whole.

"I'd like to investigate this place but it's getting late," she said.

"I know." It was a relief to Zane to leave the old town, though he was uncertain why. Avoiding the tree that had so impacted him, they found the path they'd traveled through the woods.

It was almost eight o'clock.

Time to find out who and what he was.

Chapter Nine

After unsaddling the horses and calming down the dogs, Zane raised his hand to knock on the door Lily and Charlie had used to enter the house. Kinsey caught his fist before it connected. "This is your family home, remember?" she said.

He looked down at her and smiled. "No, as a matter of fact, I don't."

"Very funny." She grabbed the knob and turned it. The dogs stayed on the porch as though they'd been trained to.

They entered a mudroom full of outerwear hanging on hooks. Racks below were stacked with boots, while a ledge above held a variety of hats. It appeared as orderly as the barn had. Judging from the size of the shoes and clothing, the space was used mainly by men.

Kinsey opened the connecting door, when once again Zane paused. Though his confidence had impressed her from the very first glance she'd had of him and had seemed to double once they got to the ranch, things had subtly shifted. Sometime earlier, back when they broke out of the woods and came across that beautiful old tree, he'd grown thoughtful and then hesitant. Even the ghost town, which she'd found fascinating, had seemed to creep him out, and if it wasn't from conscious associations, then what was the explanation? Something subconscious?

They entered what turned out to be the kitchen, a large room with two gorgeous rock walls and a wide wooden island. Lily looked up from her task at a granite drain board. The tray beside her held a dozen hollowed-out potatoes. She paused from dicing chives. "Hey, where did you guys disappear to?"

"We went riding," Zane said.

"Really? Where did you go?"

"Around."

Lily's brow furrowed and Kinsey leaped into the ensuing silence. "We rode up through the woods to a plateau and from there to a neat old ghost town."

Lily stopped what she was doing as her gaze swiveled to Zane. "You took her *there*?"

"Yes," he said. "Why?"

"No reason," Lily said, dropping her gaze. She picked up a chunk of cheese and a grater. "Chance and Pike are in the library waiting for you. Frankie drove into town, some kind of emergency or other. You know him."

"Where's your son?" Kinsey asked.

"Charlie fell asleep right after his dinner. I feed him early in the summer."

They left the kitchen without further comment. The next room was a dining room with a very long table running down the middle, set with plates and silverware at one end. Framed photographs above a sideboard caught both of their attention and they paused to look.

"That's you," Kinsey said, pointing at a dark-haired boy of about fifteen sitting astride a red horse. "And I bet that's Rose back in the day. She has to be twenty-some-odd years old."

"These other kids must be my brothers," Zane said. He pointed at a lineup of boys that ended in a man of about forty. "That must be our father," he added. "But where is our mother? There are no women on this wall."

"Or signs of one living in the house, aside from Lily, that is," Kinsey said. "Maybe your mother died some time ago and your dad just remarried."

Lily came through the door and seemed surprised to find them lingering in the dining room. She set a bowl filled with greens on the table. "If you want to talk to your brothers about something, you'd better get to it. Dinner will be ready in about a half hour. The roast is in the oven, so I have some time. Would you mind if I listened in?"

"Of course not. You seem to be an integral part of the household."

She gave him the look Kinsey was beginning to know followed almost every conversation she had with Zane. The woman knew something was wrong.

They followed her out of the dining room into a spacious entry. A broad staircase rose on the left side complete with polished banister it wasn't hard to picture Zane and his brothers sliding down when they were kids. Lily quickly led them into the library, which, appropriately enough, held shelves of books.

The only other home library Kinsey had ever seen was Bill Dodge's, with its mass of volumes that reflected his eclectic reading taste. This selection was not nearly as huge and, judging from the few titles that jumped out in a quick glance, not as varied. However, the books were not what really caught her attention.

Two tanned, weathered-looking men occupied the room. One was standing by the window with a glass of amber liquid in his hand and he turned to face them, though his gaze quickly shifted to Lily as she crossed to a bar located in the corner. He turned back to Zane and raised his glass before draining it in one swallow. There was an unmistakable devil-may-care aura about him, an edge of recklessness impossible to miss. He was easily as tall as Zane and just as good-looking in his own way.

The seated man was younger by a few years. A pair of dark-rimmed glasses perched on his nose, while longer, lighter brown hair drifted down over his eyebrows. He didn't give off Zane's steadfast earnestness or the other man's rakish quality; instead, he seemed more intense and private. Maybe it was a combination of the bookish glasses coupled with the stack of half-opened mail scattered across a table in front of him that reminded Kinsey more of a college professor than a cowboy.

These men had to be two of Zane's brothers. Though they were very different in appearance, the muscles and self-assurance emanating from all of the gathered Hastings men stood out. There wasn't a wedding ring in sight except for the gold band on Lily's hand.

"About time you decided to come home," the standing man said. "George Billings bought four hundred calves this afternoon. We need to go round them up from the Pine Hill pasture and get them to the pens for loading by Friday."

Zane nodded.

The man set aside his empty glass. "Where are my manners?" he said, his gaze drifting to Kinsey.

"What manners?" Lily mumbled without looking up.

He ignored her as he took Kinsey's hand. "I'm Gerard's good-looking brother, Chance. The quiet one on the couch is Pike. And you are?"

"Kinsey Frost," she murmured. Chance had a dazzling smile and a charming way of making a woman feel beautiful that probably got him pretty much anything, or anyone, he wanted.

However, between Chance's lingering eye contact and Zane's glare, there was enough testosterone floating around the room to fuel a rocket.

Pike took off his glasses as he stood up. His eyes were blue like Zane's but darker. "Evening, ma'am," he said. He turned to Zane and added, "Where did you run off to after Dad's wedding? One minute you were here, the next you were gone."

"That's what I need to talk to you about," Zane said. "But first of all, what do you know about the new guy you just hired?"

Lily looked up. "You asked about him earlier today."

"Yes, I did."

Pike folded his glasses into his breast pocket. "You must mean Jodie Brown. We're always shorthanded this time of year and everyone in town knows it. I guess he asked around and someone gave him our name. Why?"

"He's been here since Sunday?" Zane said.

"Yeah. I met with him in town on Saturday

evening and he said he wanted to start the next morning. What's going on?"

Kinsey took her first deep breath in quite a while. If Pike had met face-to-face with the wrangler on Saturday evening, then there was no way that man could have dumped a toolbox on her car way back in Louisiana that same night.

Zane seemed to reach the same conclusion. He took out the key chain with the Red Hot medallion and showed it to both his brothers. "You guys recognize this?"

"Sure," Chance said. "I picked that up a few years ago when I was down in Twin Falls at a farm equipment convention. You swiped it from me when I got home. Why are you asking? Don't you remember?"

Lily had been pouring drinks while the introductions were made and she arrived with a glass for Kinsey and one for Zane. Zane took a long swallow. Kinsey took hers to a chair by the window and sat down.

"No, I don't remember," Zane said. "In fact, I don't remember anything that happened before last Friday afternoon."

Both brothers wrinkled their foreheads and said, "What?" in tandem.

Zane took a seat near Kinsey. "Here's the thing. I've lost my memory. The only reason I made it back to Idaho is because Kinsey helped me trace that key fob all the way from New

Orleans. The girl at the feed store in town recognized me. I know this must sound crazy but it's true. I don't recognize anyone in this house or this ranch or this state."

"What were you doing in New Orleans?" Pike asked.

"I don't know," Zane said. He set the glass down and shifted his gaze from one person to the other. Kinsey's heart went out to him as his brothers mumbled disbelief.

It was Lily who spoke first. "That's why you've been acting so odd. That's why you rode up to the... I wondered. Does this have something to do with your neck?"

"Yeah," Zane said.

"Tell me."

Chance flashed her an annoyed look. "Aren't you supposed to be cooking dinner or cleaning something? That is in your job description, isn't it? This conversation is personal."

"Dinner is cooked," she snapped back. "And Gerard invited me."

"Leave her alone," Pike added. "Stop being a jerk."

Chance tore his gaze from Lily and zeroed in on Zane's neck. A low whistle escaped his lips. "I didn't even see all those bruises. Have you been in a fight? Aren't you always telling me to have a cool head? And what do you mean you don't know why you were in New Orleans? Why would you go there?"

"I was hoping one of you could tell me that," Zane said.

Pike sat back down on the sofa. "We don't know why you left. It's been about a week. You took off right after Dad and Grace left for their honeymoon. You looked like a man on a mission, but you didn't share any details, like why you were leaving during mowing or where you were going."

"Did I say when I'd return?"

"Not to me," Pike said.

"Nor me," Chance added.

"How about a woman named Mary or Sherry Smith?" Zane added. "Does that name ring a bell?"

"Not a one," Pike said and Chance agreed. "Are you telling us you don't remember being Gerard Hastings at all?"

"That's what I'm telling you," Zane said.

"You don't remember Dad's last wedding?"

"Nope."

"Or Grace?"

"That's the woman your…our father married, right?"

Chance chuckled. "Dad calls her lucky number seven."

"Your father has been married seven times?" Kinsey blurted out.

"Yep, that's why none of us boys really look that much alike. We each have a different mother."

"Where are they all?"

"Frankie's mom took off and disappeared a few years back," Chance said. "Mine is in Atlanta, Pike's mom lives in California with her movie-star boyfriend and his daughter."

"And Gerard's?"

"She died when Gerard was a baby."

"Wow," Kinsey said softly. "Is this new wife nice?"

"She's a little on the strange side, but at least she isn't twenty years old like the one before her. That creeped me out," Chance said.

"Grace is a nice woman," Pike added. "She's just had a hard time."

"Twenty-five years ago. Get over it already."

"There are some things you don't just get over," Lily said softly.

Kinsey saw impatience on Zane's face. This conversation wasn't answering any of the questions he wanted addressed. "Do I have a family?" he asked. "A wife, children, an ex-wife, a current girlfriend?"

"You don't remember Heidi and Ann," Pike said with an uneasy sliding glance at Chance that chilled Kinsey's heart.

Zane sighed deeply. "Who are Heidi and Ann?"

"Oh, God," Chance groaned. He backed up

until he tumbled into a red leather wing-back chair and leaned his forehead against his hand.

Pike was the one who explained. "Ann was your wife, Gerard. And Heidi was your little girl."

"Was?" Zane said. "Where are they now?"

After a prolonged hesitation, Pike sighed. "There's no way to sugarcoat this. They're both dead. Man, I'm sorry."

"When did they die?" Zane asked in a hollow voice. He'd been prepared for the possibility of his having a family, but not this.

Again, Pike responded. "Heidi died two years ago last Friday. She was six years old. Ann died the next day."

"Were they in an accident?"

"More or less. Let's talk about that later. Tell us what happened to you."

"Do you have a picture of them?" Zane persisted.

"Are you sure?"

"I'm sure."

Pike got up and walked to the desk. He picked up a framed photograph and brought it back to Zane. Kinsey leaned toward him to see the photo, though she noticed it took him a few seconds to do so himself.

It was a family portrait taken on a snowy day. Zane stood behind a lovely woman with dark hair, his arms around her waist. She held a little girl of two or three in her arms, a charmer with dimples and twinkling brown eyes.

The woman looked a lot like Kinsey.

"I don't remember them," he said softly.

Kinsey put down her untouched drink and stood up, drawing the attention of everyone in the room except Zane, whose gaze still searched the photograph in his hands. She had to get out of here. Town was less than an hour away. She could get a room for the night, start back to New Orleans in the morning.

"Tell us what happened to you," Chance demanded.

Kinsey took a deep breath. She wasn't needed here. She looked down when Zane's fingers brushed hers. "Would you mind giving them a quick run-through of the last few days while I pull myself together?" he asked.

"Not at all," she said, and knew she wasn't going anywhere, not yet, not tonight. She moved to the sofa, where Pike sat down beside her. Chance pulled his chair closer and Lily perched on the arm of the sofa near Pike. In a quiet voice, with as little drama as possible, Kinsey told them about the attacks on the sidewalk and the hospital, Zane's questions about her mother and the heavy toolbox thrown off a bridge.

"That's why Gerard wanted to know about our new hired hand," Chance said.

Lily looked frightened, of all things. "Having

someone come after you is terrifying. No wonder Gerard is jumpy."

"It is scary," Kinsey agreed. "But as far as the wrangler goes, the timing is wrong, it couldn't have been him."

"You're really not positive the bridge attack was directed at you in particular, is that right?" Pike said.

"Yes. We need to call the sheriff and ask what he's uncovered."

"I'm going to keep my eyes on Jodie," Chance said.

"Where's Gerard's truck?"

"No one knows," Zane said as he finally looked up from the photograph. "How did my wife and daughter die?" he asked.

Chance got up from his chair, walked to Zane's side and gripped his brother's shoulder. "Don't do this to yourself. Dad will be home tomorrow afternoon. Maybe seeing him will jar your memory and you won't have to go through this again. Give it until tomorrow."

"I can't," Zane said. "Tell me how they died. Please."

It was Pike who took a deep breath. "Heidi climbed up where she didn't belong. Something happened...we don't know for sure. Anyway, she fell. Ann tried to get to her but apparently slipped in the process and hit her head. If we'd found them sooner, I don't know. No one knows for sure."

Zane's stare was intense as he focused on one brother then the other. "Did Heidi fall from a tree? Did she fall from the one up on the plateau?"

"The hanging tree? No, why do you ask that?"

"It was just a feeling," Zane said.

"You have a thing about that tree," Chance said. "Always have."

Kinsey cleared her throat. Zane seemed too distracted to even ask why they called the big oak the hanging tree. She glanced at Lily who quickly looked down at her hands. Her earlier reaction to their ride suddenly made sense. "They died in the ghost town, didn't they?" Kinsey whispered.

"Yeah," Chance said. "That's right, they did."

UNABLE TO FACE sitting around a table and enduring any more stares and questions, Zane asked for and got directions to his own house. It turned out it was located down the road that ran parallel to the river.

"What do you think of my brothers?" he asked Kinsey as their headlights startled a small herd of deer.

"I think they're nice," she said. "What do you think?"

"They're different from each other," he said.

"I get the feeling Pike takes care of business and Chance gets into trouble whenever he can."

"Me, too," she said.

"He and Lily sure seem to dislike each other."

"Do you think?"

"Yeah. Don't you?"

"I'm not sure," she said.

He yawned into his fist. It was twilight by now, and so consuming had this day been that to Zane it felt as if a month had gone by. In the back of his head he knew that dismissing Jodie Brown as an assassin was premature, and from what he'd overheard Pike and Chance saying, they agreed. Since no one had any idea what Zane had gotten himself into, how could they judge how many people wanted him dead or even if there was a conspiracy? On the other hand, he now carried Pike's revolver.

It appeared his house was newer than the main house and less than half the size. Built partway up the gentle slope to the river, the view promised to be wonderful once daylight came.

An automatic light went on as Kinsey parked inside a carport next to a newer blue SUV. Zane was too tired and emotionally wrung out to take in many details, but as they moved to the front door, he heard animals in the nearby fields. Pike had assured him they'd been taking care of his horses, feeding his chickens and milking his cow. They might as well have told him they'd been airing out his magic carpet. Nothing had any relevance to him.

He opened the door with the key Pike had pointed out and held it for Kinsey to enter first. As usual, she carried her painting-supply tote over her shoulder and a small brown bag in her arms. It was filled with the few garments she'd purchased along the way to flesh out her limited wardrobe. Zane was still mostly living in Bill Dodge's old clothes and set the satchel and Kinsey's belongings on the bottom step of an open staircase leading to the second floor. Then he made sure the lock on the door was engaged and the dead bolt slid closed.

Kinsey had been flipping on lights and now he looked around the house, straining to remember anything, yearning to feel a flicker of recognition that would bring his family back into focus. He'd dreaded the house being a mausoleum filled with pictures and sadness, but it wasn't like that. Instead, it had a kind of male clutter that felt comfortable, and though there was a picture album on the table, it was mercifully closed. He wasn't up to looking at faces he should remember.

He turned abruptly at the sound of Kinsey's inhaled breath. She was staring into the living room, a comfortable-looking space with overstuffed furniture and lots of golden pine. What appeared to be an antique grandfather clock occupied one corner, while the other held a locked gun cabinet.

But what had caught her attention hung over the unlit fireplace. For one crazy moment, Zane wondered how Kinsey's likeness had made its way into his house. In the next instant, he realized it wasn't her. The woman in the painting was taller, less curvy.

"It's uncanny how much I look like Ann," Kinsey said under her breath, but he heard her.

"It's quite a coincidence," he said.

"Is it?"

He stared down at her. For days she'd been the eye of the hurricane for him, his compass. He'd grown to respect and like her. More, he'd started to envision a life with her, had wondered if love began with this aching desire never to be apart. He'd wanted her with him in every sense of the word. Finding out about a dead wife and child had jarred him and now it was clear, it had jarred her, too. He could see it in her eyes. "Of course," he said. "What else?"

"Don't you see?" she whispered.

"See what?"

"You were drawn to me because I look like your dead wife. Think about it. You were injured two years after her death almost to the day and the first woman you see who isn't a doctor or a nurse is someone so similar…"

"No," he said, grabbing her arms. "No."

She put her hands on his and leaned her forehead against his chest. "It's okay," she whispered. "It's not your fault."

He put his arms around her and held her so close he could feel her heartbeat. He'd been afraid of losing her because he was already committed. To lose her because a wife he couldn't remember was dead seemed the ultimate irony.

He tilted her chin and looked down into her eyes. He wasn't sure what he could say, but he did know what he could do. He lowered his face until their lips met. The kiss had a bittersweet quality to it that was new. Then suddenly he realized what was wrong. It was a goodbye kiss.

He pulled himself away and when her eyes opened to stare up at him, he claimed her lips again, and this kiss wasn't tentative or sweet or shy. Holding her around the waist, he lifted her from her feet, burning away her doubts and her hesitations, or at least trying to. He needed her, he wanted her, nothing had changed except everything, but that didn't affect the way he felt about her.

"Let me go," she finally whispered.

"No," he said. "I can't."

"Not forever, Zane, just for now. Put me down. Please."

He set her back on the floor and cupped her face in his hands. Staring deep into her eyes, looking for her soul, he whispered to her, "You

have to understand something. Even when I remember my wife and our daughter and what
happened to them, even when specific grief for
them returns, I will continue to have the memories and feelings I have made these last several
days with you. Those feelings won't be lost when
the others return."

"You don't know that for sure," she said.

"Yes, I do."

They looked at each other as the big clock in
the corner ticked off the seconds.

Finally, she sighed. "Let's just go to bed. Let's
put this day behind us and figure things out tomorrow. Pike said your father will be back in the
afternoon and maybe he'll know something that
will help. For now, let's not talk or try to figure
anything out except where to sleep."

He reluctantly loosened his grip and nodded.
He picked up their bags and they climbed the
stairs together.

The first room they investigated turned out
to be a time bomb. It had obviously belonged to
a small girl partial to bunnies and unicorns. He
and Kinsey exchanged stricken looks. Without
saying a word, he closed the door on what had to
be Heidi's room. It didn't look as if it had been
changed since the last time the child hopped
out of bed.

The next room appeared to be a home office,
the one after that the master suite. The room

was stuffy. As Zane deposited their bags on a bench at the foot of the bed, he noticed a picture of himself and Ann on the dresser. Judging from his image, it had been taken several years before. Where had he met her? Had they married right away? How long had they been married before Heidi came along? Had they been happy?

He laid the photo facedown. She'd been gone from the world for two years. Contemplating where he was in the process of letting her go was futile.

"I can't sleep in here," Kinsey said.

He turned to find her staring around the room. "Because of me?" he asked.

"No, because of…Ann, I guess."

"Yeah. I feel the same way. There's one more door farther down the hall. Let's see if it's a guest bedroom."

The door opened onto a room very similar to the master room. It, too, had an attached bath. It was slightly smaller, nicely decorated and a little more intimate. "Will this do?" Zane asked Kinsey.

"It's perfect."

He withdrew Pike's gun from the back waistband of his jeans and set it on the shelf next to the bed, where it would be handy in case it was needed. Kinsey took the first shower and then it was his turn to stand under the hot, cleansing water. They climbed into the king-size bed at the same time. Within seconds, they'd rolled to the middle and embraced.

He'd steeled himself against succumbing to his feelings for her. The day had been so raw for both of them. But the fact was, he couldn't control his body or his imagination, either. He'd wanted to be with her since the night they'd met and now he knew he was free. But did she know that, too?

"Have you ever been in love, Kinsey?" he whispered.

"I thought I was once."

"With Ryan, that guy you told me about?"

"No, not him. It was back when I was twelve. The boy was thirteen. He didn't even know I existed. I thought he was very mysterious."

"Maybe I should try ignoring you," he said, kissing her ear. His fingers ran over the pearly satin of her shoulder.

She drew her head back to look at him, although he could barely even see the whites of her eyes. "I don't think you need to worry about attracting my attention," she said. "And you're plenty mysterious enough, as it is."

He kissed her again, this time on the lips. He didn't expect her to respond, but to his surprise she returned the kiss with the softest lips on earth. And when she parted them for his tongue, his whole body jumped to attention.

"Slow down," she whispered against his neck.

Was she telling him to back off? If so, something had to give. "This isn't going to work," he said softly as his hand slid over the tantalizing rise and fall of her waist. "I can't lie in the same bed with you and keep my hands to myself."

"I don't want you to keep them to yourself," she said, and as she spoke, she positioned her body closer to his, fitting her hips against his. She picked up one of his hands and moved it to her breast. "I just want you to slow down." Her warm breath against his skin drove him crazy.

Her hand slipped down and brushed against an erection he was powerless to contain. There was a layer of cotton between his flesh and her hand, but he was pretty sure he was about to spontaneously combust.

He brought his mouth down on hers again as he massaged her breast, delighting in the way her nipples grew hard. He tentatively lifted the strap holding up her orange gown and she moaned deep in her throat. With her help, he slipped the gown from her supple body and wished he'd left the lights on so he could see her.

But it was enough for now to just feel her. She slipped her hands under his boxers and pulled on them. Soon he was naked, too, and any thought of slowing down was obsolete and naive.

Deep, long, intense kisses led to exploration. Her curves felt mesmerizing under his fingers, and when he touched her intimately, she shuddered. Groans escaped his own lips and her fingers ran over the steel rod of his erection. The sound seemed to add fuel to an already enraged fire. Pressing kisses down her neck, he cupped the dense soft weight of her breasts. Before he could lower his mouth to suck on her nipples, she'd clasped his rear and slid a leg under him. He mounted her quickly, delirious now with sensations. Plunging himself inside her seemed to be the most natural thing in the world, and the way she raised her hips to accept him drove another nail in his ability to delay the inevitable.

Obviously, he'd made love before. He had no specific memories of doing so, but he had been a father. At that moment it was impossible to believe there had ever been anyone else, and as they moved together, all tangible thoughts ceased.

Their release came swiftly, thoroughly, both of them crying out in ecstasy before crumbling together.

After a few minutes, he switched on a small bedside lamp, anxious to see her face, hoping he would detect no regret. He found her staring up at him from the tumble of blankets at his side, her hair messed, her eyes dark and soft.

If what he felt throbbing in his heart and running through his veins wasn't love, what was? He reached for her and she came.

Chapter Ten

Kinsey woke up the next morning to find herself naked and alone in the bed. She'd slept in, but instead of jumping up, she lay there a few minutes basking in memories of the long night until she sighed deeply, sat up and looked around the room.

The vaulted ceiling rose high over her head while sunlight poured through the windows she'd opened during the night. The room was decorated with dashes of red, the curtains fluttered in the breeze. She thought back to the master room they'd abandoned, to the pile of male clothes tossed in a chair and the half-full glass of water on the nightstand that to her signaled Zane had left the ranch in a hurry the last time he'd slept in this house.

So, what had happened at the wedding or right after it that made Zane leave abruptly? Or had he been planning to go and stayed just long enough to see his father take wife number seven?

She spied her art tote on the bench at the foot

of the bed. Yesterday had been the first day in years that she hadn't sketched or painted anyone. She'd thought about it when she glimpsed the pain hiding behind Lily's smile. She'd also thought about it when she entered the library and saw Zane's brothers. They were unique and yet cut from the same cloth. She couldn't wait to find out what Frankie, the one who had been absent, was like.

But she'd also thought about painting when she looked at the mountains, the fields, the horses. The ghost town begged to have its secrets revealed, though its worst secret of all, the deaths of Zane's family, made that impossible for her to even contemplate. For the first time in her life she ached to paint more than faces.

If she and Zane managed to get over the obstacles fate kept throwing their way, and if they managed to live through the assaults until the perpetrator was found, could she settle here?

This place was so different from New Orleans. Quieter, lonelier, the air dry instead of moist. The sky seemed three times as big, and the river, instead of being wide and lazy and muddy, was narrow and ambitious and cool. There would be snow in the winter and turning leaves in the fall. Spring would bring mountainsides of wildflowers, and everywhere you looked, at least on Hastings land, you would find cattle and horses. She'd even seen deer grazing in a meadow on the ride home from the ghost town, then again last night from the car. She'd glimpsed hawks soaring up in the sky and rabbits scurrying through the underbrush.

But the differences ran deeper and it wasn't just the scenery or the weather. Zane had grown up in that beautiful old house with four brothers and an endless stream of stepmothers. She had grown up in a series of cheap housing with one ever-present mother and no men. She'd always had something to eat and warm clothes, but she hadn't had acres of land to roam, dozens of animals to care for, a lifestyle set in motion since before she was born. She had never belonged to a piece of land, but Zane had and still did. This was a family ranch and that meant the family worked it.

After a shower, she dressed quickly, borrowing some of the cream she found on the vanity to soothe her sunburned face. Riding around yesterday afternoon out in the full sun without protection hadn't been the best idea she'd ever had. Then she went in search of Zane. She found him seated behind the desk in the room set up as an office. He looked up as she paused at the doorway and smiled at her.

"Morning, sunshine," he said as he got to his feet and approached her. The lazy, sexy look in his eyes, coupled with his loose-jointed gait, made her heart thump around. He paused right in front of her and lifted her chin. "You have a rosy glow this morning."

"I have a sunburn," she said, but she was thinking that she would never get tired of the way his eyes devoured her. Did feelings like that last? Zane's father had just taken his seventh wife. Did being raised in that kind of atmosphere encourage the concept to be content with one woman?

Why was she even thinking like this?

He lowered his head and touched her lips with his. All the emotions and sensations of the night before came flooding back, begging her to believe in fairy tales and forever. She allowed her head to dip slightly so she could brush her cheek against his knuckles.

"You look great," she told him. "I like the clothes."

He glanced down at his white shirt and the suede vest he wore over it. He hadn't shaved and the slight stubble glistening on his face beguiled her. "I found a walk-in closet full of my stuff," he said. "I seem to have a thing for vests."

She smiled as she recalled the first time she'd seen him. He'd been wearing a pliant leather vest and she'd admired the way it made his shoulders and chest look supremely powerful. And last night, aroused and commanding, the true depth of his strength had flooded her senses.

"I want to talk to you," he said. "Come sit

down." He led her to the chair at right angles to the desk, whisked a yellow baseball cap decorated with an embroidered orange dog off the seat before sitting down in front of the computer.

"Have you remembered something?" she asked.

"No. But it's weird looking at the plaques on the wall, reading emails from people who are strangers, finding things like a baseball cap abandoned on a chair that I must have left there but have no memory of doing. It got a little overwhelming, so I called Sheriff Crown back in Louisiana. At least I remember what he looks and sounds like."

She shifted her weight forward. "Did the kids confess to throwing the toolbox off the bridge?" she asked.

"Nope. In fact, they have an iron-tight alibi."

"Did he question anyone else?"

"Yes, but got nowhere. He's convinced a local is involved but admits it's strange no one seems to know anything about it. He says 'pranks' like that usually get somebody talking, but so far, nothing."

She drummed her fingernails. "So the attack might still have been aimed at you."

"For all the good that supposition is doing us. Oh, and I also called Detective Woods."

"Did he mention if anyone fitting Ryan's description turned up the victim of a crime?"

Zane settled his hand on hers. "I asked. There's been no one. Hopefully, your friend is safe."

"Don't forget he might be your friend, too."

"I'm not forgetting," he said. "Anyway, I gave Woods my real name. He's going to search hotel records and see if he can find some trace of me. He has the make of my truck, the license plate and VIN numbers, so he'll check out the police impound yards, too, and call your phone if they find it. I have to admit that makes me nervous, though."

"Why?"

"Who knows what incriminating evidence might be lurking in my truck. I'd like to think I'm an innocent victim in all this, but I can't know that for sure until it's proven or I regain my memory. I just want to be there when the door is opened for the first time."

She sat forward. "Does that mean you're going back to New Orleans?"

"Eventually. How about you?"

"Pretty soon," she said. No matter what the future held, she couldn't just walk out of her apartment or family responsibilities. Besides, she needed some space and he did, too, whether he admitted it or not. Her place was at her own home while he needed to reestablish his identity here. This was all happening too fast.

A giant pit in her stomach warned her that

parting with him was going to be pure unadulterated misery, worse now that they were lovers. By the time another few nights passed, how would she ever be brave enough to give him the space he needed?

"By the way, I found a notebook with my passwords in it, so I took a look at my bank records. I also found files in one of the drawers and scanned those. The upshot is that this is either a very profitable ranch or I am one hell of a financier. I can pay you back everything I owe you and help you replace your car."

"Don't worry about that right now…"

"Please, for the sake of my pride, just accept what I'm offering. This issue has been bugging me since the beginning. I have a nice fat checking account and a book of checks and I intend to repay you. Meanwhile, I own the SUV down in the carport, so let's pay the extra fee and turn in the rental to the local branch today or tomorrow. I'll buy you a plane ticket whenever you want to go home. Just let me know."

"Thanks," she said. Money, or rather, the lack of it, had been preying on her mind. It was a relief to know Zane could help. In a perfect world, she could gallantly refuse his offer and chalk generosity up to improving her karma; in the real world, she could not.

Her phone rang, which jarred them both. She

got to her feet as she glanced at the screen. "My mother," she informed Zane. "I'd better take it."

He picked up the yellow baseball cap and pulled it over her hair. "I don't want you burned to a crisp today," he whispered. "I have plans for you tonight." He followed this with a kiss before pulling down on the brim. "I want to go back to the ghost town. Will you go with me?"

"Of course."

He smiled. "Talk to your mom. I'll go find the kitchen and rustle us up something to eat."

She punched on the phone as Zane left the room. It was amazing how empty a space could seem once he'd vacated it.

"Hi, Mom," she said, steeling herself for more ultimatums.

"Are you still in Idaho?"

"Yes. I'll be flying home soon, maybe as early as the weekend."

"What happened to your car?"

"A small accident. How are things with you?"

"Bill isn't doing well. He refuses to go back to the hospital or even allow me to call his doctor."

"Oh, man," Kinsey said. "He sure went downhill fast, didn't he? Can Mr. Fenwick convince him to let you get help?"

"James says Bill actually has a right to conduct his death on his own terms. He has a point. It's just so scary."

"How about his nephew?"

"He disappeared again yesterday, but it's too much to hope it's for long."

"That's a lot for you to handle. How are you dealing?"

"James is a rock, thank goodness, since you're still off with that cowboy. You are, aren't you?"

"Yes. He rediscovered his identity but not his memory. Do you have a pencil handy? I want to give you the home number of my friend." She rattled off the number on the desk phone. "Cell reception is iffy here. Call me and leave a message if something happens, okay?"

"Okay."

They soon hung up. The conversation had been subdued, but it hadn't been antagonistic, for which Kinsey was grateful. A growling stomach reminded her she'd missed the last couple of meals. Time to find Zane and discover if he could cook.

"YOUR FATHER WILL be home after lunch sometime," Lily told Zane. She was up to her neck in green beans and canning equipment. Already processed quart jars lined a towel-draped table, while a big pressure cooker released steam as a timer ticked nearby. A dozen sterilized bottles, one with a wide-mouthed funnel resting atop, awaited the pile of beans Lily chopped into two-inch pieces for the next batch.

"Do you know where my brothers are?" Zane asked her.

"Over getting the pens ready for the roundup on Friday. They said you should join them if you had the chance."

"You'll have to tell me how to get there," he said. She did and told him to take truck keys out of the mudroom. Zane asked Kinsey if she wanted to come with him and hesitated when she declined. "Go have some time with them," she said. "Maybe it will help you remember something."

"I don't like leaving you alone," he said as he squeezed her hand.

She gestured at Lily. "I'm hardly alone. Listen, I promise I'll stay right here at this ranch until you get back, okay?"

"I won't be long." He kissed her cheek and squeezed her hand.

"You two are close," Lily said after the door closed behind him.

Kinsey smiled. "You can tell?"

"He's letting you wear his lucky hat."

Kinsey had all but forgotten the yellow cap still perched on her head. "I don't think he remembers it's special."

"I know, but it is. He played Bulldog Football during high school. Anyway, I'm happy for both of you. He's a good man."

"I know," Kinsey said.

"It will be wonderful for him to have children again."

"I know he wants them very much," Kinsey said. "It seems to be a part of who he is."

"Is it part of who you are?" Lily asked with a swift glance.

"A family has never been a priority," Kinsey admitted. "Until now. Last night...well, yes, I think I'm finally beginning to understand the whole circle-of-life thing. Zane is teaching me. I mean Gerard."

"I don't mind what you call him," Lily said with a smile.

Kinsey had surprised herself with her answer and for a moment felt a stir of panic. What if she built her dreams of a shared life with this man at this ranch and it never came to be? How would she go on?

And yet, what choice did she have but to see it through? Her heart had already traveled where her brain was afraid to tread.

Lily screwed a cap on a jar. "This batch will have to wait until I take care of Charlie and deliver lunch to the crew."

"How about the lunch? Can I make some sandwiches or something?" Kinsey offered.

"I already made chili and corn bread, and when I get back from running Charlie up to catch the bus, I'll grill chicken."

"That's a feast! What crew are you talking

about?" Kinsey asked as she perched on a nearby stool.

"Sometimes they burn pastures after the grass is harvested for feed. It purifies the soil. It also, I might add, works up an appetite."

"I didn't see any smoke."

"You wouldn't. The field is over the mountain, miles from here. I don't know, maybe I bit off more than I could chew today. I shouldn't have tried to can this morning." She scurried to the staircase and hollered, "Charlie? Hurry up."

Kinsey heard the little boy protest, but Lily repeated her command before resuming her task.

"Have you been working here long?" Kinsey asked.

"About six months."

"Then you didn't know Zane's, I mean Gerard's, wife, Ann?"

"No. She was already gone by the time I came. I hope Harry's new wife can make it a home again, but from what Chance says, she's got issues of her own."

"Like what, do you know?"

"I've just overheard people talking. I guess she lost her family in a series of tragic events. That was a long time ago, but she hasn't really mended. I gather she feels responsible."

"That must be terrible."

Lily looked down at her hands. "Yeah. Guilt is

an awful thing to live with. You'll like Gerard's father, though."

"What's he like?"

"Strong willed and opinionated, not my favorite traits in a male, but he took me in when I had nowhere else to turn. He's never even asked me to explain…things. Anyway, he's a chauvinist, sure. It's easier to dismiss in a man of seventy than it is in someone Chance's age."

"Explain something to me," Kinsey said. "Are you and Chance enemies or are you guys closer than you're letting on?"

Lily shrugged. "He wanted to date…I don't know."

"You didn't?"

"No. I've had enough of men like him. You know, all bluster and ego. He reminds me of… well, never mind, it doesn't matter."

Charlie tumbled into the room looking resigned to his fate. He glanced at Kinsey, then around the room. "Where is Uncle Gerard?"

"He's out working," Kinsey said. She turned to Lily. "I can drive him up to catch the bus for you."

"I appreciate the offer, but he'll require his daily pep talk," she replied. "If you could take the beans out of the pressure cooker when the timer goes off, that would really help. Oh, and the charcoal for the chicken is all laid out in the grill near the garden. Would you light it for me in about fifteen minutes?"

"Of course."

"Charlie, get your lunch box out of the fridge," Lily said as she grabbed her keys. She looked back at Kinsey and added, "Just use those tongs to lift the bottles out of the cooker and set them on that towel like the others, but make sure you wait until the pressure is at zero. I'll loosen the rings later. Thanks a bunch."

And with that, mother and child disappeared out the door.

Kinsey sat down at the table to wait for the timer to announce the pressure cooker was ready to open. The big room was humid from steam, but not entirely unpleasant. The minutes ticked by peacefully as the house seemed to settle around her. She thought back to the scrambled eggs Zane had made her for breakfast, and the way he'd flirted with her. Sharing a cup of coffee at his sunlit table in his very own house had seemed enchanting to Kinsey, like a piece of the giant puzzle called life had slipped quietly into place. There went the panic alarm again, and she smiled at her contrary thoughts.

She'd slipped her small purse across her shoulder that morning, and now she opened it without removing it from her body, taking out the book Bill Dodge had given her to help pass the time. It really was a beauty—he'd outdone himself on the binding. She opened it and found that he'd written something on the inside page. "For Kinsey," she read. "Remember, life is like a book—the important stuff happens between the covers."

She chuckled at the double entendre. Would she ever see him again? Suddenly she felt as if she was half a world away, living among strangers...

She turned a few pages until the timer finally went off. After fitting the book back in her bag, she opened the lid and carefully lifted the dripping bottles one by one. When they were all lined up without their shoulders touching, she began the search for matches and found them in a drawer by the stove.

It was warm outside but not as humid as inside the house. The three dogs ambled over as she walked to the garden, where she found a large chimney-style fire starter filled with newspaper and coals sitting on a bigger bed of charcoal. She'd seen these used before and knew the object was to light the newspapers and wait until the coals on top caught fire, then spread those over all the others.

This was going to take a few minutes, so after she lit the newspaper, she decided to investigate the garden. She let herself in the tall fence that must have been constructed to keep deer from munching their way through the produce.

Though she didn't close the gate, the dogs held back. One wandered off toward the barn and the other two followed him.

It was a pleasure to walk the well-tended path. Rows of cornstalks and pole beans climbing up their strings heightened the feeling of isolation. Bright red tomatoes hung from trellised plants, while rows of peppers, eggplants and vines covered with cucumbers covered the raised beds. Yellow marigolds added color and beauty. She'd never been alone in such a lush, productive garden and found it tantalizing.

What would make it perfect, she decided, was a shade tree and a bench. How wonderful would it be to sit out here and read a book or try painting a still life…

Surely no one would deny her a tomato or two? She looked around until she found a branch covered with grape-sized fruit, and stripped three juicy specimens to pop in her mouth. The urge to find a basket and harvest everything in sight was overpowering.

Well, since she couldn't pick the fruits and vegetables, she could do the next best thing. She could draw them and luckily she'd brought along her art tote when they left Zane's house that morning. She turned toward the gate with the intention of grabbing a sketch pad and charcoal pencils but stopped short. A man stood a couple of feet away. A smile died on her lips as he raised his hand and revealed an ugly black gun.

"Who are you?" she gasped. "What do you want?"

His tongue darted over what appeared to be thin lips, although it was impossible to know for sure because of the reddish beard that covered half his face. Jodie! He shot a quick look over his shoulder as though he'd heard something. When he turned back to her, he licked his lips again. "You're coming with me," he said.

She wanted to run or scream but could do neither. It was as though her feet had grown roots in the fertile earth, holding her in place. He jabbed the barrel against her stomach. "Just do as I say," he snapped. His expression had gone from nervous to intense. He took a deep breath. "Listen. If you're good and quiet and don't give me any trouble, he won't have to watch you die. If you piss me off, he'll never forget what he sees."

He? Zane?

"What have you done to him?" she cried.

He grabbed her arm and pushed her in front of him, twisting her elbow behind her back. The gun poked against her spine. "Walk ahead of me. Don't try anything." His rough nails grated against her skin. She took a few steps and he stayed glued to her back.

"Hurry up," he demanded.

"Tell me what you've done to him!" she pleaded

as they exited the garden. She frantically cast her gaze around the ranch, praying someone would see them and intercede. There just wasn't anyone. The dogs had reappeared and stood nearby, watching with big brown eyes. The only thing that moved was the flame shooting out of the coal chimney.

"Walk over to that blue truck."

A rusted truck sat a few feet away, a squat, windowless canopy secured to the bed. "Open the door," he demanded as he waved the gun at the passenger side. Maybe she'd have a chance to escape when he went around to get behind the wheel.

Or maybe he'd shoot her right here and now. But why? To get to Zane? It had to be. "What do you want?" she repeated as she opened the door. "Just tell me."

He pulled her back against his chest, raised the gun to her temple and hissed hot air against the back of her neck. His body felt as hard as a concrete pillar, the arm wrapped around her waist as unyielding as a steel cable. "Did you honestly think Block would let you walk away?" he said. "Did you think he wouldn't find you, that he wouldn't hunt you down? Did you think he'd let you steal the only thing in the world he cares about?"

"Who is Block?" she cried. "I don't know who you're talking about."

"Don't play dumb with me," he said. Her pulse seemed to jump against the cold metal as he guided the gun down her neck, slowly and methodically, down between her breasts, to her belly. She struggled to breathe, to think. Every nightmare she'd ever had shot through her head. "You are about to have a very fatal accident," he whispered. "And after you're dead, Block will get what he wants, what is his."

"I don't know anyone named Block. Please."

"You're playing with me," he growled against her skin. "That means I play with you, too." He abruptly thrust his tongue into her ear, his free hand twisting the strap on her purse up around her neck. She grabbed at his hands to keep from being strangled and threw her head back into his, hoping to knock him out cold. His teeth came down hard on her earlobe and she screamed.

"Bitch!" he barked as he pushed her against the truck.

Warm blood dripped down her neck. She tried dodging away, but he caught the strap again and yanked it hard. Then he brought the gun down on her head. She raised her arm to protect herself. "You're making a mistake," she screamed. "Stop!"

The next blow connected with her temple. She tried to grab something to steady herself, but she couldn't make her fingers work. Her body hit the ground with a thump. A gray rock filled her entire field of vision until it, too, faded away.

Chapter Eleven

Zane found his brothers where Lily had told her they'd be. Both were working on the pens located in the middle of a vast field surrounded by acres of sloping hillsides. He understood that the pens, shoots and ramps would be used by a group of cowhands to gather and contain cattle, to sort and load them onto trucks so they could be taken to their new home, though he had no actual memory of ever doing any of the work himself.

Chance told him to shovel aside the deadfall and debris that blocked several of the gates while he replaced a rail. "It's odd giving you directions when you've been doing this stuff your entire life," he said with a wink. "You're the oldest, you're usually the one bossing everyone else around."

"Yeah, well, I'm not exactly myself," Zane said.

Pike tossed a broken board into the back of his truck. "Still can't remember anything, huh?"

"No." He wiped the sweat from his forehead with a handkerchief and added, "Have you ever heard me mention anyone named Ryan Jones?"

Chance paused mid–hammer stroke and appeared to think. Eventually he shook his head. "No."

"How about you, Pike?"

"Can't say as I have. Who is he?"

"Someone in New Orleans. A friend of Kinsey's. It doesn't really matter. But let me ask you this. Didn't it seem funny to you guys that I would leave the ranch during a busy time of year and right when Dad had just gone off on his honeymoon?"

Pike shrugged. "Sure it did. You're usually not the secretive type. But you've organized things here pretty efficiently and we have adequate help."

"I organize things around here?" Zane asked.

Chance laughed. "Like I said, Gerard, you're kind of bossy."

The name still sounded like a character out of a book to Zane. He dug in his shovel. "What about our father?"

"He thinks he's the brains, but he's been deferring to you, and to a lesser degree the rest of us, for years. Man, he isn't going to believe you don't remember any of this."

Zane glanced up at the blazing sun. Why in the world had he worn a vest? He glanced at the watch he'd put on after finding it on top of his dresser that morning. "As soon as we're finished here, I need to get back to Kinsey. I don't like leaving her alone."

"That's fine," Pike said. "Tomorrow we're going to round up the rest of the calves over at the Bywater pasture. We could use your help."

"Sure," Zane said. Maybe Kinsey could borrow a pair of boots from Lily—they looked about the same size. Then she could go with them.

"Anyway, you don't have to worry about the new wrangler, Jodie," Pike added. "I sent him and a few others up to the ridge to bring down the herd and sort out the calves. They're getting really big. It's a good thing we found a buyer."

"So Jodie isn't on ranch land?"

"Well, define ranch land," Pike said. "This place is strung together like a patchwork quilt. We own most of it, we rent some of it, we lease other parts. Anyway, just rest assured, Jodie is about ten miles south of here and won't be back for hours."

"Even if he wasn't, no one gets past our iron maiden," Chance said.

"What iron maiden?"

Pike threw another piece of wood. "That's what Chance calls Lily."

"That's one of the names I have for her," Chance said. He hammered in a nail on the gate he was repairing and added, "I also call her irritating, defensive, secretive…in fact, if she wasn't so easy on the eyes, she'd have no redeeming qualities."

"She's got a cute kid," Zane offered.

"Charlie's okay. A little wimpy, maybe. How he got that way with Lily for a mother is a mystery."

"Dad likes Lily," Pike said. "So do Frankie and I. You're the only one with a problem."

"Frankie is the youngest, right?" Zane asked. "Is he back on the ranch today?"

"He didn't show up," Chance said. "Frankie isn't exactly dependable."

"He's trying to change," Pike said.

"He needs to try harder," Chance grumbled.

Zane concentrated on his job for a few minutes, but a growing sense of uneasiness made it hard. He didn't want to walk out on a job half done, so he redoubled his efforts until a half hour later, the last rail had been replaced and the gates were all operational. "I'm heading back," he announced.

"I'll ride with you," Pike said as he tossed tools into the back of the truck.

Chance banged in another nail. "I'll be right behind you guys. I want to finish up here first."

Zane let Pike drive as it was obvious his brother knew the lay of the land a lot better than he did. "Last night you called that big oak up on the plateau the hanging tree. Why is that?" Zane asked as they set off toward the ranch.

"Because of the three men who died hanging from its limbs."

"Three? When did this happen?"

"A long time ago." Pike slid him a look. "You saw the ghost town. It used to be a pretty prosperous mining town. Then four men robbed the bank the night a big payload came in. The citizens formed a posse and ran them down. They brought them back to that tree and hung them up to die. Their bodies weren't cut down for months. And after that, the town died."

"Yikes," Zane said. "But you mentioned four thieves."

"One of them, a guy by the name of John Murdock, escaped. The story goes he got away with all the money and was never heard from again."

"Chance says I've always been obsessed with that tree. I don't know if it's true, but I do know I had a profound reaction to it yesterday and I've dreamed about it a couple of times."

"Everyone but Dad and Chance get the willies around the tree. The whole town calls us Hanging Tree Ranch, not Hastings Ridge. But in your case it runs deeper than that. A bunch of older boys tied you to the tree when you were about ten. As I've heard the story, it took Dad until the middle of the night to find you and by then you'd been stuck for hours listening to coyotes, absolutely terrified. That leaves an impression."

"No kidding. Do we own the ghost town?"

"Yeah. You've been lobbying to plow it under for obvious reasons. Dad wants to take it apart board by board and resell the lumber to a decorator in town. Apparently there's a market for old wood."

His voice trailed off and Zane figured it was because he didn't want to reopen the subject of Ann and Heidi, but he soon realized he was wrong. His brother had let up on the gas pedal. His gaze followed a dust trail going down a road running at right angles to the one they were on. Pike glanced at Zane.

"That looks like Jodie's old beater truck."

"Are you sure?"

"Pretty sure."

"But you sent him miles away from here."

"Exactly. He said nothing about not going. This isn't the road we typically use to get off the land. It leads up into the hills, eventually to the ghost town. I can't imagine what he's up to, but he came from the direction of the ranch. Maybe he went there to tell someone he was moving on. Drifters do that, you know. Let's go check out the house. Jodie might have said something to Lily. We could clear this up in a minute or two."

Zane turned in his seat to watch Jodie's truck racing away in the other direction. They picked up speed as the road evened up and within ten minutes were parking by the garden next to the SUV they'd driven from Zane's house a couple of hours before. Zane was struck with the horrible feeling he was too late, but too late for what? He jumped out of the truck before it came to a full stop. "Kinsey?" he yelled as he ran. He tore through the kitchen door. The room was empty and quiet, still filled with jars of beans and little else. He stood still for a second, then yelled Kinsey's name again. The silent building seemed to hold its breath and he knew in his bones she was not inside this house. A shiver snaked down his spine.

He hurried back outside right as Lily pulled her red car to a stop. The smile slid off her face when she looked at Zane and Pike. "What's wrong?"

"Kinsey isn't here," Pike said. "Did she say anything to you about leaving?"

"No. She promised—"

"Look at this," Zane interrupted. A yellow baseball cap lay on the ground. The cap was jarring enough, but even more alarming were the scuff marks in the dirt and the fresh tire tracks leading away from the ranch.

"That's your Bulldog hat," Pike said.

Zane picked it up. "Kinsey was wearing this." He turned it over in his hands but froze when a bright red smear along the band caught his eye.

The two brothers exchanged a one-second stare before they both sprinted back to the truck. Pike got behind the wheel, gunned the engine, made a wide turn and took off back down the road, turning when they came to the spur that would put them on Jodie's trail.

Enough time had passed that the dust had died down, making it anyone's guess if Jodie had continued up this road or not. All Zane could think of was that red smear and he looked at it again. His gut and every other instinct in his body told him this was Kinsey's blood. He couldn't imagine how the hat would end up in the dirt unless it had been torn off her head, a possibility supported by those ominous scuffle marks in the dirt. It was inconceivable to him that she would have lost it without knowing. And there was that blood...

"We'll find him," Pike said with a slap on his shoulder.

"I know." He looked out the window at the rolling hills and felt sick inside. Jodie could be almost anywhere. Maybe they should call the police and try to get some help.

"If they took her to get to you, then she may be the bait in a trap," Pike said.

"It doesn't matter," Zane said. He'd been staring out the window as he spoke and now he sat forward. "Slow down, Pike. Go back a few yards."

Pike backed up the truck. Two tracks of flattened grass led off across a field, their bent stalks shimmering gold in the heat. Pike immediately followed the trail.

"What do you figure? He's got a good twenty-minute lead?"

"At least," Zane said. "Probably more like thirty minutes. Is it possible he's headed to a major highway?"

"It's possible. It's a little out of the way but definitely possible, especially if he thinks we might be following him."

The land began to climb until they finally flew over the top of the ridge. Zane recognized the plateau they'd ridden to the day before. Up here the ground was harder to read, rockier and scattered with downed trees and gullies. There were no longer any clear impressions of tires to follow.

Off in the distance, gazing past clumps of trees, he could see the imposing shape of the huge old oak. "I have a feeling about that tree," Zane said.

"Then we'll go look," Pike said as he veered that direction. They had to slow down because of the rocks, but Pike kept with it. Zane leaned out the window and tried to see something, anything that would help. Was he letting the creep factor of the tree get to him? "Kinsey, Kinsey," he whispered into the wind, then he sat up straighter. "I see something blue under the shade of the tree."

"Big enough to be a truck?"

"Yes. It's not moving. Why would he park there?"

Pike didn't answer, but Zane could easily come up with a perfectly innocent answer. Maybe the guy was eating lunch in the shade of the tree. Maybe Kinsey was back at the ranch somewhere. Maybe he'd jumped to conclusions...

The ground finally evened out and they were able to travel faster. The blue truck was growing more defined, as was a figure moving around beside it. By the size of the person, Zane knew it wasn't Kinsey, so it must be Jodie. If the guy was just out for a ride, he'd stay where he was and find out what all the drama was about. That seemed to be the case for a few seconds, and then suddenly the man disappeared around the back of the truck. When he reappeared the next time, he was climbing into the driver's seat. The truck wallowed over the roots before it took off, making a wide circle to head south.

"I can intercede his path," Pike said and slowed down to make a wide turn.

"No," Zane said quickly. "Something's on the ground. Drive to the tree. Hurry."

Pike aborted his turn and they all but flew over the remaining distance. Try as he might to discern what Jodie had left behind, the intense shade of the tree and the twisted depth of the roots concealed the truth. Pike finally hit the brakes a good distance away to avoid those roots and Zane popped open his door. He ran with his heart in his mouth and then stopped abruptly as the ambiguous shadows on the ground evolved into Kinsey.

She lay sprawled, her clothes bunched around her body, her hair almost covering her face, smaller in this state than he'd ever seen her, her skin delicate and pale and covered with blood. For one interminable moment, he thought she was dead, but then he heard her moan. A second later, he knelt by her side.

Pike came to a grinding halt beside him. He, too, kneeled. "Oh my God," he whispered. "What did he do to her?"

Zane felt her hands. They were cool to the touch. He smoothed her hair away from her beautiful face and saw that her right earlobe was torn. She cried when he tried to pull down her shirt and straighten her legs. Her eyes fluttered open and she looked at him. Tears immediately trickled down her cheeks.

"Where does it hurt, baby?" he whispered.

She licked her lips.

"There's water in the truck," Pike said and ran off to get it. Zane slipped off his vest and folded it under her head. He tried once again to make her comfortable, checking for broken bones as he did so, finding to his relief that a majority of the blood was on her face and seemed to come from the torn lobe and a gash across her forehead.

Pike was back in a minute and they wet a handkerchief to drip warm water onto Kinsey's lips. She'd drifted off for a few seconds, but as the water touched her, she opened her eyes.

"Zane?"

"I'm here, honey. What happened?"

"A man," she said.

"It was Jodie. Did he hurt you anywhere I can't see?"

"My ribs," she said very softly. "My head."

"You're okay now," he said. Who the hell *was* Jodie? And why had he taken Kinsey and then abandoned her here? What was the point?

In a way, he didn't care. Kinsey was beaten and bloody because of his selfish desire to have her close to him. He would find Jodie and one way or another, exact revenge for what the man had done.

But there was another question just as compelling. How had he, Gerard Hastings, provoked such violence? He had to find out. Someone had to know.

First things first. "Come on, sweetheart," he murmured to Kinsey. "We need to get you to a doctor."

She looked into his eyes but didn't speak. Together, he and Pike helped her stand, then Zane scooped her gently into his arms. Pike wandered away with his cell phone as Zane carried Kinsey to the truck. The back was too full of tools and discarded lumber to use it as a bed for her, so he carefully helped her settle in the front seat, then he scooted in after her. She collapsed into his arms as Pike got behind the wheel. Pike handed him Kinsey's shoulder bag, her wallet and the small art book. "I found these tossed aside," he said. "They're hers, right?"

"Right," Zane said as he took the proffered items. "Who did you call?"

"Chance. He's taking off to look for Jodie."

"If he finds him, the bastard is mine," Zane said.

KINSEY KNEW SHE was safe and for the moment that was enough. The cocoon of Zane's arms lulled her as the truck ambled along slowly in deference to her injuries. They finally hit smooth pavement and the speed increased.

The urgent-care facility contacted the police. By the time they showed up, Kinsey's ribs had been taped, her forehead gash closed with the proper bandages, her earlobe stitched and her body laced with antibiotics and a tetanus shot. She was told in no uncertain terms that she should go home and go to bed at once, that in a bigger city with an actual hospital, she would have been admitted for at least an overnight stay.

"Hey, Gerard, long time no see," Officer Robert Hendricks said as he came into the treatment room. The two men shook hands. Kinsey thought the officer's expression reflected a certain surprise at Zane's lack of response to his overt friendliness. "Where's Pike?" he added. "I heard he came in with you."

"He did. He got a call from Frankie, who's been in town a couple of days for some reason. Sorry, I'm unclear on the details."

"You don't know why Frankie is here in town?"

"No, do you?"

"No, but I better look into it. Damn, I hope he hasn't slipped back into trouble." He turned his attention to Kinsey. "Are you up to telling me what happened?"

She was sitting in a reasonably comfortable chair, her hand firmly clasped in Zane's. It was impossible not to notice the way the officer's gaze kept straying to their linked fingers.

"It started in the Hastingses' garden," she began. All she could think of was Jodie's threat. "He told me if I came quietly, Zane would not have to see me die, but if I caused a fuss, Zane would never forget how Jodie killed me." She swallowed a lump and took a deep breath. "Then he started in on someone named Block."

Zane took the floor for a moment and explained what they'd already been through in New Orleans. He also confessed his amnesia. "The Block name means absolutely nothing to me," he added. "I'll ask Pike and the others about it when I see them."

Hendricks nodded as though a light had gone on in his head. "You have amnesia?"

"Yes."

"Well, that explains why you're looking at me like we've never met."

"I'm sorry," Zane said. "How well do we know each other?"

"High school, college, you were my best man, my wife and I were Heidi's godparents."

"Oh, hell," Zane said. "I'll buy you a beer when I get back to normal."

Hendricks laughed but soon turned serious again. "Okay, Ms. Frost. What did Jodie say about this Block?"

Jodie's voice came back, as did the sensation of his hot, sour breath against her neck. It was the exact words that were jumbled and she shook her head in frustration. "I can't remember exactly how it went," she admitted. "The impression I got was that Block was angry with me for taking something that was special to him. Jodie said I would die in an accident and then Block would get back what was his. It was all so confusing. Up until then I thought this all revolved around Zane...I mean Gerard. When I said I didn't know anyone named Block, Jodie got angry. He...he ran the gun down my chest... I don't know, I thought for a moment he was going to rape me. I tried to get away. He bit my ear. I don't remember anything after that until he pulled me out of the truck. He took my handbag and he tore it apart as I tried to sit up. He took the cash, but there was hardly anything left. I wondered if this was some kind of bizarre robbery, but the money seemed incidental to him. He threw all my things into the field and started yelling at me."

"What did he yell?" Zane asked.

"I don't know. He was impossible to understand. The kicks began and I just tried to protect my head. After a really hard blow to my side, he said he was going to find a rope in the back of his truck and tie me to the tree for the buzzards." She glanced up at Zane. "I thought about you finding me like that, what that would do to you." Unbidden tears burned behind her nose. Zane hugged her shoulders and smoothed her hair.

She took a deep breath. "But all of a sudden, he gave me a last kick, got in his truck and left in a hurry. I couldn't believe he was going away. The next thing I knew, Zane and Pike were there."

"Does anyone have a picture of him?" Hendricks asked.

"If you have a piece of paper and a pencil, I might be able to give you something better than a verbal description," Kinsey said.

"She's a portrait artist," Zane explained. "A very talented one."

"My lucky day," Hendricks said as he hustled out of the room to find supplies.

AFTER LEAVING HIS family at the ranch, Zane drove on to his house where he helped Kinsey up to the second floor. She sat gingerly on the bench at the foot of the bed while he carefully removed her clothes. Black-and-blue marks had begun to appear, each one representing a punch or a kick. He clenched his jaw so she wouldn't see how angry they made him.

"My orange gown—"

"I'll get it for you." He found the garment beside the bed where he'd tossed it the night before after almost ripping it from her body. He pulled it over her head and helped her into the bed.

"You're safe now, you know that, right? I'll be here," he told her as he helped her find a comfortable position and covered her with a light blanket.

She caught his hand. "I want to go home," she said. "I don't want to be here anymore."

He swallowed his disappointment. Of course she wanted the comfort of her family and her own four walls, but the doctors had told him she shouldn't fly for a few days. He leaned over to kiss her forehead. "I'll take you home any time you say," he whispered against her cheek. They would drive. It wasn't as if they hadn't made the trip before. "We'll leave tomorrow if that's what you want."

"That's what I want."

"Okay, sweetheart. That's what we'll do. Try to get some sleep."

Her grip tightened. "You aren't leaving me, are you?"

"Of course not," he said. He wanted to add that he would never leave her side again, but he wasn't certain that would strike her as an attractive thought. Maybe leaving here meant leaving him.

Within a few minutes, her grip grew slack, her breathing even. The next thing he knew, he was opening his eyes on a room where the light had significantly changed. He glanced at the clock and sat up. He'd fallen asleep sitting up and over two hours had passed. He stood when he realized what had woken him was the sound of an engine outside.

His first instinct was to grab the gun off the shelf, and he did this before creeping across the heavily shadowed room to the window. It was crazy to think Jodie would dare come back to the ranch, but his heart beat in his throat anyway. Then he recognized Pike's truck. He tucked the gun in the small of his back and raced downstairs to open the door before Pike could ring the bell and disturb Kinsey.

"How is she?" Pike asked as he came through the door.

"She's asleep right now, but I wouldn't be surprised if she has nightmares about this for weeks."

"I'm real sorry. I feel bad that I hired that jerk. I should have insisted on references. We've never had trouble before, so I guess I got complacent."

"You didn't know any of this was going on," Zane said. "In retrospect, I should have hunted him down last night and I shouldn't have left Kinsey behind—"

"We both feel responsible," Pike interrupted. "And it does Kinsey absolutely no good at all."

"I know it doesn't. She wants to go home. I can't let her make the trip alone."

"I understand," Pike said. "We'll get along without you. Dad is home now, he plans on riding out with us to Bywater, so don't worry about it."

"I have a favor to ask," Zane added.

"Shoot."

"I need someone to take Kinsey's car to the rental place and settle the bill. Of course I'll repay it."

"I know you will. I'll take care of it. How are you going to get to Louisiana?"

"I'll take the SUV. Hopefully when we get there we can find my truck. I want to give the SUV to Kinsey since I'm responsible for the destruction of her car. Which leads me to ask something. The ranch appears to be profitable. I'm a little startled at how much money I have."

"The ranch is profitable," Pike said, "but you're twice as rich as anyone else. Your mother's father died a couple of years ago and left you a small fortune."

"That explains it."

"Like I said, Dad got home a couple of hours ago. We've filled him in on what we knew so you wouldn't have to start at the beginning again. Lily was going to come stay with Kinsey, but she got busy cooking, so I came instead. Dad wants to see you."

Zane looked toward the stairs. Reason said Kinsey would sleep through his absence and that Pike was just as capable of protecting her as he was. Nevertheless, he didn't want to leave.

"I've been meaning to ask if the name Block means anything to you," he said. "Jodie mentioned it to Kinsey during the abduction."

Pike shook his head. "It doesn't ring any bells. She doesn't recognize it either?"

"No. One more question. What's up with Frankie and why aren't any of the rest of you married?"

"That's two questions," Pike said. "It's hard

to keep in mind that you don't remember everything about us. Frankie has been in and out of trouble his whole life. I guess there's one in every family and in our family, it's Frankie."

"I thought it was Chance."

"No. Chance is a player in some ways and he never walks away from a fight, but he doesn't tangle with the law."

"And Frankie does?"

"Afraid so. He used to run with an unruly bunch of losers. Lately he's been trying to sort himself out. Listen, you have enough to worry about right now. I'll take care of Frankie."

"How about the married part?"

Pike flashed a tentative smile. "That's harder to explain. Things just haven't worked out for any of us. Maybe it has something to do with the parade of women Dad marched through our childhood. Maybe that left a bad taste in our mouths when it came to marriage."

"Yet I married," Zane reflected.

Pike looked toward the stairs. "Yeah, well, you seem to have a knack for finding exceptional women."

After the past several hours, Zane had grown to like and trust Pike. For the first time since arriving at the ranch, he thought he might be able to belong here again, to care about these people even if his memory never returned. "Thanks for all you did today," he said. "I'll go down to the ranch house, but I won't be long. I want to be here when she wakes up."

"I'll sit in your office," Pike said, "so I can hear if she needs anything."

"Thanks." He took the gun from his waistband and pressed it into Pike's hand. "Take care of her."

"I'll keep her safe until you return."

Chapter Twelve

He found everyone in the kitchen, sitting around the big maple block counter. Lily stood at the stove stirring a pot of what smelled like marinara sauce, while Charlie perched on a stool nearby watching her. Chance was sorting mail and the man who had to be his father sat as though he'd been expecting Zane.

"What the hell is this I hear about you having amnesia?" he demanded.

It was pretty easy to see parts of himself and his brothers in his father. Harry Hastings had Chance's forehead and full head of hair, though his was mostly white. On him, Pike's dark blue eyes and straight brows looked stern instead of thoughtful, and though Zane was decades younger, his father's general physique was much the same. There was also a belligerent twist to his lips that seemed to be all his. It announced clearly he didn't like obstacles and would not tolerate any funny business.

"Hello to you, too," Zane said.

Harry Hastings grunted at Zane's reply. "I heard some little gal was injured by one of our wranglers. Is she okay?"

"She will be," he said.

"Can't believe something like that could happen on Hastings soil. Damn negligent of Pike to hire him."

"Pike didn't know," Zane said. He looked around for some sign of the new wife. "Where's your bride?" he asked.

"She wanted to stay in town until she's boxed up all her stuff for the move out here. Damn woman has been living alone in a tiny house for twenty-five years. You wouldn't believe how much crap she has. Anyway, we'll take a transport and the horses out to Bywater tomorrow. I predict your memory will come back as soon as your butt hits a saddle."

"If that was true, it would be back now," Chance said. "Gerard rode out to the ghost town as soon as he got here."

Harry's brow furrowed. "Why did you go out there if you didn't remember Ann and Heidi?"

"I didn't plan on going there. It's just where we ended up."

"We?"

"Me and the woman who was hurt today. Her name is Kinsey Frost."

His dad grunted. "Well, a day working cattle will put you right as rain, mark my words."

"Actually, I won't be here tomorrow," Zane said. "Kinsey wants to go back to New Orleans. I'm taking her."

"New Orleans?" he snapped.

"That's where she lives. That's where I lost my memory. Do you know why I was in New Orleans while you were on your honeymoon?"

"No idea. You never said a word to me about it."

Zane fought off disappointment. His father had been his last hope. "Listen, Jodie Brown gave Kinsey the impression someone named Block was angry with her for taking something he cared about more than anything in the world. He told her she would die in an accident. She hasn't the slightest idea…"

His voice trailed off because his father's attention had shifted to Lily, who had stopped stirring the sauce. She stood with her mouth agape, her gaze connected to Harry's.

"What's going on?" Zane asked. Even Chance looked up from the mail, apparently sensing the same sudden tension that Zane did.

Lily licked her lips. "Did you say Block? Jeremy Block?"

"She didn't hear a first name that I know of."

"Oh my God," Lily said, dropping the spoon into the sauce and lifting Charlie into her arms. She looked around the room as if she was searching for a way out of the kitchen, off the ranch, maybe off the planet.

"Is it him?" Harry asked.

Her voice, when she answered, sounded different. "It has to be. Jodie must be one of his minions." She met Zane's confused gaze. "Oh my God, Gerard, don't you see? He thought he was taking me. He thought Kinsey was me."

"You? Then you know Block?"

Harry Hastings got to his feet. He walked to Lily's side and put out his arms. "Charlie, how about you and me go find the dogs?"

Charlie all but leaped into Harry's arms and the two of them started for the door. Lily looked reluctant to part with her son and thankful for the help all at the same time.

By now, Chance had set aside the mail and was staring at Lily. "How could anyone confuse you with Kinsey? Granted, you're about the same size, but your hair…"

"Is really brown. I bleach it," Lily said. "I used to wear it long, like Kinsey does. I wanted to look different, to disappear…he must have found her where he expected to find me." She swallowed hard. "How did he find me? I have to leave here. I have to go. Now. Tonight."

"Wait a second," Chance said as he stood. "Who is this man?"

She searched his face for several seconds before finally whispering, "Charlie's father."

"And what did you take from him?"

She seemed unable to speak, so Zane said it for her. "You took Charlie," he said. "You took Block's son."

Lily covered her face with her hands as sobs racked her body. Zane and Chance exchanged alarmed glances until Chance stepped closer. "You aren't going anywhere," he said gently. "You're safe here."

Lily looked up at Chance. "You don't understand. I'm not safe anywhere."

ZANE CLIMBED INTO BED after seeing Pike off, too wrung out from the day to even think about eating. The room was dark by now and Kinsey didn't stir when he slid between the sheets. As always, the proximity of her body aroused him. He held his hands in fists at his sides, determined not to disturb her. It promised to be a very long night.

"Aren't you going to make love to me?" she whispered.

He turned on his side. "You're awake," he said.

"I've been waiting for you. I want you to make love to me. You'll have to do most of the work, though."

"Are you sure you're up to it?" he asked as he stroked her cheek, careful to make sure it was her left one so he wouldn't inadvertently touch her bandaged earlobe.

"I'm sure. I want wonderful thoughts in my head, not ugly ones."

"I'm your slave to command," he said, sliding his hand down her throat until he hit the fullness of her breasts.

Their lovemaking was gentle compared to the night before, Zane being careful not to settle his weight on her bruised and cracked bones. He satisfied her needs and then his own, creating a pocket of potent warmth that seemed to drive away the demons. And when they both lay replete, she sighed deeply.

"I feel safe with you," she said, nuzzling his shoulder. "Tell me a story, okay? Let me hear your voice as I fall asleep."

He didn't want to tell her about Lily's revelations because he didn't want to burden her with thoughts of Jodie. That story could wait until morning. He couldn't tell her about his past because she knew as much about it as he did, but he could tell her about the places he wanted to visit. "Have you ever wanted to walk on an iceberg?" he began. "That takes a helicopter ride, I suppose. Imagine standing there on the tip of something so huge with the ocean in every direction. Or how about we travel down to Ecuador and then on to the Galápagos Islands. The wildlife there is something else." He paused for a few seconds and cleared his throat. "I've also given consideration to where we should honeymoon. How does Hawaii sound? Too ordinary? If so, maybe Tahiti or Australia or even the Bahamas. No, wait, maybe you'd rather go to Europe and visit art museums. What do you think, Kinsey?"

She didn't respond because she'd fallen asleep. He brushed her lips with his and she made a contented noise in her throat. At that moment he knew he had to have her, he couldn't let her go even if it meant leaving the ranch and his family.

Wouldn't his dad be thrilled to hear that?

It didn't matter. He'd apparently loved a woman once before, and a child, too. Fate had given him a second chance and he wasn't going to blow it.

THE NEXT MORNING, Kinsey watched as Zane packed their bags. He'd just finished telling her about Lily's amazing revelation of the night before. It was reassuring to discover she and Zane hadn't been the intended targets, though the lingering malice and fear would take a while to deal with. She must have created doubt in Jodie's mind when she said she didn't know Block. After driving toward the road, he must have decided to check out her story by searching her wallet. And then, with the arrival of Pike and Zane, he'd cut his losses and left her.

Her phone rang and she glanced at the screen. "Your mom?" Zane asked.

"Yes. I don't know if I'm up to this."

"Then don't answer it," he said. He looked back at her and his expression softened. "Do what you need to do, sweetheart. I'm going to go get some things out of the office. I'll be right back."

As he left, Kinsey answered the phone, doing her best to sound normal. "Hey, Mom," she said.

"I have news," Frances Frost announced.

"Is it Bill?"

"No, well, kind of. James has asked me to marry him right away, before Bill dies so Bill can know that I'm taken care of."

Kinsey stared out the window for a second. "Married. You're getting married?"

"Yes. Can you believe it? After all these years…"

"Mom, isn't it happening a little fast?"

"Fast? I've been a widow for twenty-five years. What's fast about that?"

"You know what I mean."

"Yes, I know what you mean. You're being cautious. But James has promised to take care of me. You have your life, it's time I allowed myself to have mine."

The statement reminded Kinsey of the time her mother had said she'd sacrificed everything for Kinsey. It was kind of troubling. "If this is what you want, then I'm glad for you," she said at last. "When's the ceremony?"

"Today. I wanted you to know."

Today! "Mom, we're actually about ready to leave for New Orleans. Could you possibly wait until I get there to, ah, share this with you?"

There was a substantial pause, then Frances spoke. "I can ask James."

"Would you? It would mean a lot to me."

"Then okay, we'll wait. But not for long, not with Bill coughing constantly."

"I'll need four days," Kinsey said. She knew they could get back in three, but she needed to have a little time to make sense of this once she got there.

"Okay. Let's say three o'clock four days from now, whether you make it or not, okay?"

"Thanks, Mom. I won't miss your big day. Is Bill's nephew still there?"

Frances lowered her voice. "He thinks I don't know what he's doing, but I can tell he's still searching the house. What in the heck is he looking for?"

"I have no idea. What does James think?"

"He says to ignore him. I'm trying. Have to go now. Keep in touch, honey, and hurry home."

Kinsey clicked off the phone and stared at the screen until Zane appeared in front of her and gently lifted her chin. "Are you okay?"

"We're going to a wedding," she said. "Mom is getting married."

"To the lawyer?"

"Yep."

"Are you good with that?"

"No. Two weeks ago she never mentioned his name. And now it's James this and James that. I'm afraid she's responding to outside influences."

"Like what?"

"Well, like my sudden desertion, for instance. And Bill's impending death. I think she's afraid to be alone."

"I imagine people marry for worse reasons," he told her.

"I guess."

"Maybe the lawyer has been lonely, too. Maybe he figures it's time to seize the day."

"You're probably right."

"I'm going to go put our things in the car. You'll feel better when you get there and see everything is okay."

He leaned down and kissed her lips and her heart raced. Every time he looked at her or spoke to her or touched her, it was more intense than the time before. She'd never felt about anyone the way she did about him. If her mother experienced even a molecule of that kind of desire, who was she to question it?

He turned at the door. "I'll be back in a few moments to help you down the stairs, okay?"

"Okay. Thanks."

As his footsteps faded, a chill ran through her body. All of a sudden she felt as though she was standing at a crossroad, buffeted by the inescapable winds of change. She hugged herself tighter.

Loss was in the air. She could almost smell it.

"I STUDIED A MAP," he announced an hour later when he left the main highway. "We're going to take as many smaller roads as possible. It might make the trip a little longer, but I'll feel better not being so damn obvious."

"But now that we know Jodie was after Lily, not you and me, what concerns you?"

He shook his head. "I'm not sure. Gut reaction to what happened yesterday. It might have been a mistake, but it served as a reminder that New Orleans could be deadly for us, and I just want to make sure nothing else hurts you. Ever."

She smiled. "Sounds good to me." She cuddled back in the pillows Zane had brought along in an effort to make her comfortable, wrapping a blanket around her legs to ward off the chill of the air conditioner.

"What did Lily say last night, you know, about Block?"

"Nothing much. Just that he was Charlie's dad. She was obviously terrified."

"Is she going to leave?"

"I don't know that, either."

"If Jodie is an example of how Block intends to reclaim his son, who can blame her for bolting? Does your father know this guy?"

"No. I asked him about it before I came home last night. All he said was that Lily was the grand-daughter of an old friend. When he heard she needed a place to retreat for a while, he offered her a job. He said it was obvious she didn't want to talk about what was wrong, so he left her alone. From what I've seen of the man, that must have taxed him. He's not exactly Mr. Hands Off."

"I hope Lily will be okay," Kinsey said before yawning into her hand.

The hours passed in a haze as she did her best to breathe in such a way that her ribs didn't hurt. After a light lunch, she fell asleep and didn't awaken until Zane announced they were getting a room at the first motel they ran into. The room they found was a lot nicer than either had expected, and the soft bed dominating the area looked like a slice of heaven to Kinsey. As always, being in Zane's arms was like a magic potion.

The day after that passed in a long, mind-numbing daze as they pushed the SUV and themselves hard.

They made it back to Louisiana by midnight

of the next day, when Zane admitted he was too tired to drive another foot. He checked them into a ground-level room and excused himself to take a shower. Kinsey looked at her face in the mirror and almost gagged. No wonder she'd been asked so many questions about her injuries. Tomorrow they would be in New Orleans and she'd be her mother's maid of honor. Wouldn't she look fetching in the wedding photo?

She groaned at the thought and then groaned again when she realized she'd forgotten to call. It was late, but even if Frances didn't answer, at least Kinsey could leave a message. She placed the call and it switched to the answering service almost immediately.

"Hi, Mom, sorry I didn't call earlier. We're somewhere around Shreveport at the Red River Inn. I'm not sure how long it will take us to get back to New Orleans because we're traveling the scenic route, but I'll call when I get there and it will probably be sometime tomorrow, so you and I will have a whole day to go shopping for whatever you need. See you soon."

Zane came out of the bathroom followed by a billow of steam. Wet dark hair framed his amazing blue eyes, and his muscles, as he walked toward her, rippled with sensuous ease beneath his bare flesh.

She raised a hand to touch the bandage on her forehead and winced. He stood over her a moment, just about blowing her mind with the bevy of hot, damp masculinity hovering just a few inches away. Her pulse pounded in her throat. He sat down next to her, his powerful thigh touching hers. It was hard to catch a decent breath. Her imagination soared at the thought of being in his arms, of having him inside her.

He lifted her hand and brought it to his lips to kiss. "Does your head hurt?" he asked.

"No worse than usual."

"Then what's wrong?"

"I don't know. I guess I just got a breathtaking eyeful of how gorgeous you are and it reminded me I look like a zombie."

He stared into her eyes and smiled seductively. "Baby, baby, baby," he whispered as he touched her lips with his. "Glance down at my lap and you will find proof positive that you look perfect to me."

She did as he asked, looked up at him and licked her lips. "Care to prove it?"

"Thought you'd never ask."

THEY GOT A good start the next morning and, as usual, Zane left the major highways in favor of subsidiary roads. Kinsey had lived in Louisiana for almost four years now, moving there after college, but she'd never traveled these more remote highways. They were running alongside the Red River on a narrow road bounded on one side by the river and on the other by a slough. There was little traffic and as they drove, huge raindrops spattered against the windshield in the sudden deluge of a summer storm.

"It's so much different here than Idaho," she said as she reached into her purse to retrieve lip balm.

"Do you like it here better?"

"I don't know. A couple of days ago, all I wanted to do was get away from your ranch. It seemed so full of recent tragedy and intrigue. And then there was Jodie... New Orleans, in comparison, seemed safe, at least to me, but now, I don't know."

He glanced at her as she took out Bill Dodge's gift book. "Have you read that yet?"

"I browsed through it a day or so ago but I haven't actually read it," she said, once again opening the cover and reading Bill's dedication. "Zane, what are you going to do when you get to New Orleans?"

"Check with Woods about my truck, make sure you're okay with your family, go to a wedding...try to find answers." He paused for a second, and then snapped, "What the hell is that guy doing?"

She looked up from her book. A big orange truck barreled toward them, straddling the yellow line.

"Is the driver drunk?" Kinsey gasped.

Zane steered the SUV toward the nearest highway edge. Kinsey glanced over the flimsy-looking guardrail to see the muddy water of the slough. The sudden downpour had caused the water to move faster than normal. When she looked back up, the orange truck was closer and still coming on like a speeding train, way over on their side of the road. She realized it was the kind people rent to move their own stuff, ten feet high and half again as long. It looked humongous.

"Hold on," Zane yelled as he turned the wheel hard to avoid a head-on collision. Their vehicle slid along the guardrail metal against metal. But as the truck loomed over them, the driver must have yanked his wheel. The SUV, with nowhere else to go, burst through the guardrail and sailed over the embankment. Kinsey gasped as they landed ten feet out in the rushing water. The current immediately swept them along even as they began to sink. Muddy water poured through the open windows.

"Get out!" Zane yelled. "Hurry."

Kinsey tried to undo her seat belt, but her hands were shaking so hard she was clumsy and couldn't get the mechanism to release. The water continued to rise, soaking the thin blanket she'd wrapped around her legs. The belt finally opened and she jerked her body around to struggle with the door, but half of her was trapped. She turned back around to find Zane. What little she could see of him was disappearing through his window. She gave up on the door as the pressure outside made opening it impossible. The car had settled in the thick layer of mud on the bottom, leaving barely an inch of air at the top of the cabin. Floating pillows and debris obstructed movement in the murky water. She held her breath. What did she have? A minute? Two, maybe?

Strong hands clamped her arm and pulled again and again. Zane, it had to be Zane. She kicked free of the blanket at last and exited the car, breaking to the surface with a sputter, amazed she could take a breath, that she was alive. The current worked against her as she held on to Zane's shirt, relying on his superior upper-body strength to gradually guide them to shore. Other motorists had stopped. Someone threw a rope that Zane caught. He clasped Kinsey around the waist with his free arm. At last her feet found purchase on the slippery bottom. Together, they climbed the steep bank, Kinsey's ribs screaming with protest. The crowd reached out to help them over the guardrail.

Zane's arms had always provided a haven and this time was no different. They stood together as the pouring rain washed muddy water from their hair.

ANOTHER SHERIFF. ANOTHER tow truck, another few hours spent answering questions. Other motorists had noticed the orange truck's erratic path. Someone reported there was no license plate on the truck. One person swore there was a single driver, another swore there was a woman sitting by his side. Everyone agreed that as soon as Zane's SUV burst through the guardrail, the truck had gunned its engine and taken off.

Zane and Kinsey went through the motions of answering question after question that led nowhere. There wasn't any doubt to Zane that they had been the target, a fact proven when the tow company found a tracking device affixed to the undercarriage of the SUV.

Kinsey had left a message for her mother mentioning alternate routes and the one they'd taken was the most likely candidate. Still, to find and rent a truck like that and get it to the right place at the right moment seemed an impossible feat. And why would her mother do such a thing?

So, was it the nephew or even the lawyer? Zane didn't know enough to connect the dots.

Another rental followed their eventual release and they drove it as far as the nearest hotel, where they took hot showers and Zane re-dressed Kinsey's wounds. He sent all the wet clothing he'd salvaged from the car once it was towed out of the slough to the overnight laundry

service and they both changed into the ubiqui-
tous terry-cloth robes provided by the establish-
ment. Zane knew that Kinsey was fading fast,
trauma heaped on trauma, wounds affected by
the latest situation. He wasn't doing a grand job
of protecting her.

In something of a miracle, the little book Bill
Dodge had given Kinsey had not washed out of
the car and Zane had been able to save it. He
spread it open on the counter in the bathroom
to dry, blotting its pages with a hand towel, hoping to salvage something of the sentiment and
beauty. He felt terrible that her keepsake was in
its current sorry state.

He heard Kinsey on the phone, no doubt calling her mother. He caught only a few words and
ducked back into the room to make sure everything was okay.

"That was James," Kinsey said. "Bill ended
up at the hospital again and Mom is with him.
James said she must have forgotten her phone
in all the confusion. Anyway, he'll pass along a
message that we're running behind schedule but
will be there for the wedding tomorrow." She set
the phone on the nightstand. "This means I'm
going to have very little time to talk her into
waiting a while before getting married."

He sat down next to her. "We'll get a real
early start."

"Okay. Did you lock the door?"

"Yes, don't worry."

A few seconds later, she lay her head back on a stack of pillows, and a minute after that, she fell asleep.

After double-checking the locks, Zane settled in the chair by the window, staring at her, thinking. If only he could remember why he'd asked about Kinsey's mother, why he'd driven to New Orleans in the first place.

As the light faded in the room, he made a decision. Kinsey's mother must have the missing pieces of the puzzle. She might not know she had them, but his gut was telling him she did. It no longer mattered to him that she didn't want to talk or that it was her wedding day or anything else.

Tomorrow, he would find out what she knew or die trying.

Chapter Thirteen

"Wake up, sweetheart, we're almost at your place."

Kinsey roused herself from a restless nap and opened her eyes to find they had finally made it to New Orleans. She'd drifted off while examining Bill Dodge's book and it sat open in her lap. Though Zane had done a good job of trying to salvage it, she suspected it was a lost cause. The glue on the paper attached to the inside cover had been damaged and had begun to curl away. She touched it idly as she stared out the window and felt a bulge beneath her fingertips. Carefully, she peeled back the paper and withdrew an envelope with her mother's name written in water-stained blue ink.

"What's that?" Zane asked.

"Something for my mother. This is Bill's handwriting. He must have sealed it inside this book when he rebound it. I don't know why in the world he didn't tell me it was there or what it's all about, but I'm glad I'm seeing her today to give it to her."

"Maybe you should open it," Zane said. "After all, it was in a book he gave you."

"No way," Kinsey said. "I learned at an early age not to tamper with my mother's privacy. Hey, I wonder if there's anything in the back of the book." She flipped it over and lifted the cover. The paper had begun to peel away here, too, and she helped it along.

"Anything?" Zane asked as he slid a glance her way.

"Another piece of paper," she said as she unfolded it. This one didn't fade, he must have used a different ink."

"What is it?"

She was quiet for a second and then almost laughed. "It's a map of his house. It shows a secret room behind the bookcase in what was once his library. There's a red *X* as in *X* marks the spot. This must be where he hid everything. Good heavens."

Zane whistled. "Crafty old guy, isn't he?"

"Yes," she said, and placed the unopened letter and the treasure map within the pages of the book. For a second she stared out at the familiar streets. She'd changed more in the past week than she had in the past ten years and nothing looked or felt the same. Especially not the police car parked in her driveway. She and Zane got out of the rental and waited while a uniformed policeman approached them. "Is this your place?" the officer asked Kinsey as his gaze traveled between her wounds and bandages.

"Yes. What happened?"

"One of your neighbors reported hearing a noise last night. When they checked this morning, they found your door open and called us."

"Has anything been taken, can you tell?" Kinsey asked.

"You'll know better than we."

As he spoke, another car arrived and Detective Woods got out. "I heard about this on the police radio," he said by way of greeting. He shook Zane's hand and then demanded to hear what had happened to Kinsey, whistling when she and Zane finished their explanation. "Good heavens."

"Any word of Ryan Jones?" she asked him.

"None. How much do you know about him?"

"Not much. He apparently lied to me about where he worked."

"Chances are, if he lied about that, he lied about other things. He might be a con artist of some kind."

Kinsey glanced over at Zane. She knew he was still wondering if he and Ryan had been involved in something dicey—heck, so was she.

Woods addressed Zane. "We found your truck. It was in a parking garage. They waited seven days before calling us. We towed it to the impound yard."

"I'll come and retrieve it later today," Zane said. "Kinsey's mom is getting married in a few hours."

"The ceremony won't take long," Kinsey said. She couldn't picture them all sitting around and chatting afterward.

"Come see me after you get your truck," Woods said. "We have still shots taken from video both on the street and in the hospital. You can't see a face in either one, but maybe one of you will recognize something familiar that can help us identify the culprit or culprits. The wife and I are having a party this evening, so can you possibly make it before five? After we're done, you're welcome to follow me home, if you like. My wife makes a mean gumbo."

"Sounds great," Kinsey said.

They all climbed the stairs. Kinsey went inside first, but she didn't make it more than a few steps. It was obvious the place had been searched, less obvious if the intruder had found what they were after.

"Offhand, it just looks like someone was looking for something hidden in a drawer or under a carpet," she said.

"That's how it strikes me, too." Woods gestured at the paintings on the walls. "Did you do these, Ms. Frost?"

"Yes."

"I had no idea you were so talented."

Kinsey murmured her thanks as she glanced at the faces gazing down from the walls. Strangers, most of them, at least their inspirations were. The art itself had become more real than the subjects they depicted. And yet, somehow, those faces weren't front and center in her life anymore. Now she thought of Charlie's shy smile, Lily's haunted eyes, Pike's bespectacled intelligence and Chance's grin. And Zane, of course. Always Zane.

Eventually, the police left with admonishments not to stay in the apartment until the locks were fixed, an unnecessary warning. They changed clothes and Kinsey packed a few things to take with her. She had access to the owner's garage and Zane found boards and nails to secure the door.

He looked sophisticated and sexy in the tan suit he'd had laundered after their dip in the slough. It fit him perfectly, enhancing his broad shoulders, the crisp white collar framing his wonderful face. Kinsey chose a floral dress she hadn't worn since buying it months before. It fell in soft pleats to her knees, and the corseted midriff helped bind her ribs, making sitting and bending easier. She'd done her best to camouflage her injuries by carefully arranging her hair over her forehead and right ear. Zane's lingering appreciative glance reminded her of the first time they'd actually met and the way his blue eyes had delved right inside her soul to take up residence.

"I'm not going to try to talk her out of getting married," Kinsey said. I'm going to give her Bill's letter and all the other papers and keep my mouth shut."

He was quiet for a second before he spoke. "Kinsey, think about it. Regardless of the map, Bill writes your mother a letter of some kind and then binds it into a book he made a point of giving to you along with a cryptic inscription that could be interpreted as encouraging you to figure out how to find what he's hidden. Maybe what's in that letter is not something he wanted your mother to see while he was still alive. You may be doing her no favor by handing it to her on the brink of her wedding."

Kinsey opened the party purse into which she'd shoved the bare essentials, including the papers. What Zane said made sense. "You're right," she said, and slipped the stiff papers out of the envelope.

"Anything legible after being in the water?"

"Barely. It's a letter, all right. There are actually two pages—oh my, the second one is a will."

"Bill's will, I take it."

"Yes. It looks as though he's left everything

he owns to my mother. It says something about betraying her trust and hoping she can forgive him. Here's something about retribution…" She scanned the letter quickly, her heart pounding as she began to make sense of what she read. "He says the house is full of treasures that he hid when his nephew started coming around and he had…doubts about something…no, I can't read what he had doubts about. There's something here about Mr. Fenwick…knowledge, it says. The rest of the words are blurred, but I get the feeling Bill is saying Fenwick knew about his plan to hide things. My God, Zane, if James got wind of this will then he would know my mother is about to be a very wealthy woman. Is that why he's been pursuing her so intently?"

"It sounds like it," Zane said as he pulled up in front of the Dodge house.

"Zane, do you think this had anything to do with what happened to you?"

He shook his head. "I don't see how, but it's awfully coincidental I was asking about her before someone tried to kill me. I'm not sure why I didn't pursue this more aggressively a week ago. You might not have been hurt…"

"Finding out who you really are was part of the process of getting to this point," Kinsey said. "Don't be so hard on yourself."

He put a hand over hers. "We have to warn your mother carefully, Kinsey. For lots of reasons."

"Yes, you're right."

"Don't put those papers back in your purse. If Fenwick catches on that you have them, that's the first place he'll look. He could very well have searched your apartment, you know. Tuck the papers in your dress somewhere."

She didn't take time to think how silly it was to do it. She just rolled the papers and the map and stuck them down in her bra. "How do you like my new curves?" she asked while batting her eyelashes.

He leered at her a moment and smiled. "I think I like the old ones better."

A NEIGHBOR MUST have been having a party, because there was simply no parking close to the house. They found a spot a half block away and walked, holding hands. Loud rap music blared from the party house across the street. Zane thought it would add an interesting twist to the middle-aged wedding about to take place.

James Fenwick answered their knock. "Come in, come in," he said. He was dressed in khakis and a knit polo shirt. Zane felt instantly overdressed, but perhaps Fenwick hadn't changed into his wedding duds yet. "You finally made it," he added.

"Yes." Kinsey looked around the foyer. "I'm sorry we're late. Where is everyone?"

"I have very sad news," he said, his expression growing somber. "Bill passed away. I didn't want to tell you over the phone."

Kinsey tightened her grip on Zane's hand. "Oh, I'm so sorry," she said. "He was a wonderful man. I hope it was peaceful."

He nodded. "It was."

"Where's my mother?"

"That's the other thing I have to tell you." He closed the door, clicked the dead bolt and encouraged them to move farther into the house. He spread his hands as he continued. "Your mother and I decided to get married when we saw how quickly Bill was slipping away. Don't be upset with her, it just seemed like the right thing to do. She's afraid you'll be disappointed. Well, you know Frances. When she's uneasy, she cooks. She's making a big lunch. Come on back to the kitchen."

They followed him through the living room, where he pushed open the door leading to the old-fashioned kitchen. He gestured for Kinsey to enter before him. He followed close on her heels. Zane was taller than either of them and could easily see over their heads.

The only other time he'd been in this room it had gleamed and sparkled. Now, dirty dishes littered every horizontal surface. A narrow door across the room stood ajar. There was no sign of Frances.

"Where's Mom?" Kinsey asked.

"I don't know," James said.

"Why is everything so messy?"

James seemed flustered. "It's been hectic here lately. I could have sworn she was in here cooking."

"Where's Bill's nephew?" Zane asked.

"He went out."

"Are you sure?"

When James didn't respond, Kinsey called out. "Mom?"

There was no reply, but the open door beckoned Kinsey. "The basement is down there," Kinsey said as she flung it wide open. "Mom?" she called. "Are you down there?"

Zane moved to her side. "Remember your ribs," he said. "Let me go look."

"The light switch doesn't work," Kinsey said as she flipped it on and off with no effect.

"Must be a fuse," James said. "I'll try to find a flashlight. If she's fallen, she may need help right away." He called out, "Frances, can you hear me?" to no avail.

"I can see well enough to get started," Zane said as he took the first downward step. The first half of the steep stairs were sided on both sides by solid walls outfitted with a handrail. About two-thirds of the way down, one wall stopped abruptly, but there was still a railing for support on the open side. Zane had expected the light to improve at this point, but it didn't. He paused to look back toward the kitchen. Kinsey stood framed in the light at the top. "Tell James to hurry with that flashlight," he called.

Instead of answering him, she turned and suddenly James loomed beside her. It appeared they struggled. Zane started to climb back up to help. Before he could take more than a couple of steps, Kinsey shot toward him, her hands grabbing for the railings, her feet working overtime to catch up until the inevitable happened and she missed a step. A second later, she flew into Zane. Her momentum sent them both crashing against the open railing that broke under the onslaught.

They landed six feet below in a heap of humanity and splintered wood.

KINSEY RAISED HER HEAD and looked down at Zane's slack face. He'd taken the brunt of the fall and seemed to be unconscious. She moved off him and checked him as well as she could in the very poor light. "Zane, honey, wake up." He didn't move, but at least his breathing sounded steady and his skin felt warm. Was her mom down here, too? Why was it so dark? Had someone covered the windows?

She crawled to the wall where she could leverage her weight to stand. Gasping as her ribs protested, she clearly recalled James ripping her bag from her shoulder and shoving her down the stairs.

Was it possible he had also shoved Zane into the street over a week before? Of course it was.

Everything that was happening had to revolve around this house and its hidden treasures and her mother's inheritance. At least she could still feel the papers against her skin, but where did Zane fit into it?

Her phone had died in the slough, but what if James had acted impulsively and then run away? Maybe she could just walk upstairs and use the phone to summon help.

The lights came on suddenly, just about blinding her. She looked up the stairs to see two men standing in the open doorway. She quickly ducked out of sight. The men at the head of the stairs started speaking.

"Did you search her apartment? Was it there?" It didn't sound like James.

"Yes, I searched… no, I didn't find anything," James replied.

The other man swore. "I leave for a couple of days and look what happens. Did you even check Hastings to see if he was carrying a gun before you pushed him down there?"

"Give it a rest, Kevin. Everything is fine. You don't carry a gun to a wedding and that's where they thought they were going."

"But they missed out, didn't they?" the other man said. "I knew you'd marry the old broad before Dodge took his last breath. Had to make sure you were in her will, didn't you? It hasn't shown up, so now you got married for nothing. The house will come to me, just as we originally planned."

"And I'll get half," James said.

"Sure," the other man said breezily as the stairs squeaked. They'd begun their descent. Kinsey looked for a place to hide but stopped abruptly when she saw Zane. There was no way she'd leave him unprotected. She couldn't see her mother, but there were a couple of ancillary rooms down here. Maybe they'd locked her in one of those.

"I'll be a widower by midnight," James added. "And let me remind you that we wouldn't have to get rid of all three of them if you'd done a proper job of it in Shreveport. Either time, I might add."

"You're the one with connections up there. You were part of the legal team for Chemco, not me. You should have gone and done the dirty work. Besides, you had two chances to get rid of Hastings, too, and you bungled both of them."

"Not my fault. I had to act fast when I heard Hastings asking about the Dodge housekeeper. No time to plan things properly. And the hospital attack would have worked if that damn nurse hadn't shown up when she did."

The men paused where the railing had given way and stared down. Kinsey did her best to meet their gaze with defiance. She saw that the new man was younger than James and carried a gun. Even from six-plus feet away, she could see the arrogance burning in his green eyes.

"Kinsey," he said. "Wish I could say it was nice to see you."

In that instant, she recognized his voice. But the man she associated with that voice had curly blond hair and dark brown eyes. "Ryan?" she said, confused.

He shook his head. "Kevin Lester, alias Ryan Jones, alias Chad Dodge. Heck, by now I answer to almost anything. Go ahead, call me Ryan."

"What's going on? Where's my mother?"

He stepped off the last stair and looked down at her. "How about a kiss for old time's sake?" he asked and started to claim one.

She slapped him. A piece of his beard came loose and dangled from his chin.

He reached up and plucked it off. "Hair dye, applications, optical contacts…you can learn a lot in prison if you pay attention, and I did. That's where I met Bill Dodge's real nephew. By the time I got out, I knew more about Chad Dodge then I did about myself. When Chad overdosed, I was able to convince Bill Dodge I was his long-lost nephew."

"Until you got cocky and aroused his suspicion," the lawyer chided. He looked at Kinsey. "Bill asked me for guidance. He didn't trust his nephew, so he'd hidden all his valuables, but he wouldn't tell me where. I told him to tread gently because his nephew had a hot head but that I would hire a private investigator and have Chad verified. Of course I did no such thing.

"Anyway, Bill was determined to change his will to benefit his loyal housekeeper. He wanted advice about how to protect her inheritance if it was proven she'd committed a capital crime. That got me curious, but about then he stopped talking. He wouldn't even let me draw up the will, said he'd do it himself and make sure it was safe."

"Crime?" Kinsey asked. "My mother a criminal? What in the world are you talking about?"

"That's what I wanted to know. That's why I sent *him* to get friendly with you," Fenwick said with a nod toward Ryan. "When that didn't work, I decided to warm up to Frances."

"And then we lucked out," Ryan boasted.

"That's right," Fenwick said, nodding. "I hardly ever go in that little grocery store down the road, but there I am one afternoon when Hastings waltzes in and starts asking questions about Mary Smith and the Dodge housekeeper. I had to know why he was interested in your mother, so I stole his wallet and phone. Thanks to that, I was able to figure out where Hastings was from and that narrowed my search. I finally figured out what was going on and I knew that if Bill Dodge made Frances his beneficiary, she needed to stay lost to the world at least until she made a will of her own. Hastings had to go."

"But you guys screwed that up," Kinsey said softly.

"Yeah, well, once we found out Hastings had amnesia and that you and he were getting close, it seemed like we might skirt by until Bill died, Frances inherited and she died. Then we could disappear substantially better off than we are now."

"You had to make sure my mother married you before she knew about the money. Otherwise, she'd leave most of it to me."

"Exactly."

Kinsey was determined not to ask this man what he thought her mother had done that would land her in jail. If Frances had committed a crime, it went a long way toward explaining why she'd spent Kinsey's life looking over her shoulder, restless and suspicious. Kinsey wanted answers, but not from this jerk.

Ryan nudged Zane with his foot. "Time to wake up, sleepyhead."

Zane groaned as his eyes flickered open. He tried to sit. Kinsey knelt to help him. Ryan grabbed her arm and pulled her away. "Leave him down there. Fenwick, check for a weapon."

A moment later, Fenwick finished a quick search. "He's clean."

"Where's my mother?" Kinsey demanded.

"In the washroom," Fenwick said over his shoulder.

"You'll have time to catch up while we wait for it to get dark," Ryan said. "James, get the tape."

James took a roll of duct tape off a nearby shelf. As he did that, Ryan put a stranglehold around Kinsey's throat. "You, Hastings, get up nice and slow or the lovely Ms. Frost won't live long enough to say goodbye. Walk over there toward that closed door. There's a washroom back there. Move it."

Zane shuffled off in the commanded direction. Kinsey was afraid another head injury following on the heels of the first had exacted a devastating toll. He opened the door to the small room full of laundry equipment and one other human. Her mouth covered with a strip of tape, ankles bound together and hands secured behind her back, Frances sat on the floor by the washing machine, her eyes growing huge as she looked from Kinsey to Zane and then to James Fenwick.

With the gun still pointed at Kinsey, Fenwick taped Zane the same way he had Frances except for the mouth, and then it was Kinsey's turn. He tore the tape from Frances's lips. "Yell all you want, dear wife. It's a big old house, no one will hear you. You have some explaining to do to your daughter before you reach the pearly gates."

"After it's dark, we'll take a road trip to the swamp," Ryan said as he turned off the overhead light. "Friend of mine owns an alligator farm. You'll love it there. At least, at first you will." And he closed the door.

Chapter Fourteen

The only light in the small room came from the front-loading dryer after Zane managed to open the door that activated the interior bulb. Then he and Kinsey took turns trying to release each other's wrists, but the tape just stuck harder the more they struggled. Frances sat nearby, oddly subdued.

"Mom?" Kinsey said. "What's going on?"

"James is a maniac," Frances said. "I've been down here for two days. He's convinced Bill left his house and treasures to me. That's what he and that phony nephew of his have been looking for. A will."

"We have it," Kinsey said.

"You do?"

"Bill gave it to me. Zane and I found it this morning."

"Well, it doesn't matter now," she said. "James and I signed wills leaving everything to the other right after we were married."

"We also found a letter Bill wrote you. It was

meant to be an apology because he'd betrayed your trust and told Fenwick the truth you'd confided in him. What truth, Mom? I don't get it."

"I do," Zane said.

Kinsey turned to face him. "Really, Zane? You've figured it out?"

"Most of it. There's something else. It's time to start calling me Gerard."

She stared into his eyes, suddenly understanding the difference she'd sensed in him after he recovered from the fall from the stairs. "Your memory is back?"

"Splotchy but improving. You two scoot as far over there as you can. I'm going to be making some noise."

"It won't help," Frances said. "This part of the basement is as good as soundproof."

Kinsey scooted over, as did Frances, when it became clear Zane didn't intend to yell for help. Instead, he raised his bound legs and brought his shoes down on the open dryer door. He did this four or five times, then took a rest, breathing hard for a moment. "I know why I was in New Orleans," he said with a glance at Kinsey over his shoulder. "I remember who sent me and why." His gaze shifted to Kinsey's mother. "It was to see you, Frances."

She shook her head.

"Your daughter sent me."

Kinsey jerked. "I sent you? Huh?"

He twisted his body around to face her. "Kinsey, I suspect this woman's true name is Mary Smith. She's not your mother."

"What are you talking about?" Kinsey said, looking from Zane to Frances.

"Right before my father's wedding, his bride showed me a letter she'd just received. It was from a man in New Orleans who used to know her family. He swore that he'd seen Mary Smith in his neighborhood. He didn't know what name she was using, but he had heard that she worked for a rather well-known man in the area, a guy by the name of William Dodge."

"This has nothing to do with me," Frances said. "Kinsey, don't listen to him."

Zane continued as though she hadn't spoken. "Trouble was, Mary Smith was supposed to be dead. Grace had to know the truth, but she didn't want to tell my father. She begged me to come look into it. That's why I drove here. To find Mary Smith and hopefully, a girl named Sandra."

Kinsey could feel the shakes starting in her body's core. "Sandra?"

His voice grew gentle. "Mary Smith is your grandmother, not your mother. She shot and killed your father, kidnapped you and disappeared from Idaho. Then she arranged your fake deaths so the authorities would stop looking for her. That's why your life was so nomadic, that's why she was always anxious. She's been running for almost twenty-five years. Your given name is Sandra."

Frances had buried her face against her bent knees.

"Wait a second," Kinsey said. "Your new stepmother is my...my mother?"

He nodded.

"But I have a birth certificate and a social security card saying I'm Kinsey Frost."

"Frances, don't you think you owe Kinsey an explanation? You can't hide from this any longer."

Frances looked up. Her tear-stained face terrified Kinsey. "It's true," Frances whispered. "After I...took you, I got a job caring for a sickly baby about your age. When she died, I stole her identity and gave it to you. I changed my name so we'd match and just avoided situations where I had to prove who I was. I did it because I had to."

"You had to?" Kinsey repeated. "Why?" She blinked back tears. "Why?"

"To save you," Frances whispered.

"Save me from what?"

Frances shook her head and pressed her lips together.

Kinsey's throat tightened. "I can't hear any more right now," she said, and then in an abrupt turnaround added, "What about my father? I mean the one who died in a bus crash."

Frances took a shaky breath. "Your grandfather died years before you were born. I had to give you a father. When I read about the unidentified man on the bus, I decided to use him."

Unspent tears burned behind Kinsey's nose. Everything was made up. Her name wasn't her name. Her birthday wasn't real. Her mother wasn't her mother, the father she'd mourned had never existed. "I don't believe any of this," she whispered.

Zane looked at her again. "I'm sorry, Kinsey. I wish it were different. I have to keep trying to break this door."

"I know," she said.

Once again he raised his legs. Kinsey could only imagine the strain and stress of what he was doing as time after time his feet slammed down on the dryer door. The machine was old, but the hinges held.

He took breaks now and again, scooting next to Kinsey, putting his face close to hers. As time passed and the hope of creating some way to cut their bonds began to seem increasingly remote, he whispered into her ear, "I want you to know I love you," he said. "If we survive tonight, I want you to be my wife."

"But you must remember Ann and Heidi now. Are you ready to move on?"

"I never thought I would be," he said. "I thought I'd just hurt forever. And then I met you. I know we both need time to…adjust to everything. I just wanted you to know how I feel. I hope you feel the same way." He kissed her gently. "I can't bear the thought I might ever lose you."

"You won't," she said. "Never."

"Okay, love. That's settled. Now, this is what we're going to do. We're going to sit back to back and use each other to get to our feet. Can you do it?"

"I'll try."

It was harder than she thought it would be because of the muscles she needed to use that were connected to her cracked ribs, but stifling a scream of pain, she managed. "Now what?" she said.

"I'm going to sit on that damn door and you're going to sit on my lap."

With that, he dropped himself down hard on the dryer door. Kinsey inched her bound feet close to join him, but it proved to be unnecessary. The door groaned and ripped off of the machine. Zane fell with it to the floor. Sure enough, the metal hinge had torn away from the dryer and jutted out in all its snaggletoothed glory just waiting to saw through some duct tape.

"You go first," Kinsey said. Zane managed

to get on his knees and back up to the busted hinge. A minute later, he was free.

"Now what?" Kinsey said as they all stood. They'd removed most of the tape, but Frances had been sitting for over two days and hadn't eaten or drunk anything in that long, as well. Moving stiffly, she drew a handful of water out of the laundry faucet and drank it down like it was champagne.

Zane caught Kinsey staring at Frances and wondered what she was thinking. Having just recovered the memories and emotions, both good and bad, that define any individual, he considered what was worse: to have no memory of what you'd lost or to have to redefine everything you thought you knew. He hoped he could help her see that many of the people and things she'd believed in were still real, but he knew it was going to take her time to work through it all. At least she wouldn't have to do it alone.

He glanced at his watch and saw that it was almost six o'clock. Darkness was still hours away. "Is there another way out of the basement?" he asked.

"Just windows," Frances said. "You'd have to break them, they don't open."

"And they must be boarded up," Kinsey added.

"I'm going to look around," Zane said. "You

two stay here." He didn't miss the uneasy look that passed between the women as he turned the knob on the door. It had been locked from the outside. Shoving his shoulder against it, he applied thrust and weight and heard the gratifying sound of an old lock giving up.

The lights were off in the basement, so he moved slowly to avoid running into something. He wouldn't chance the stairs for the simple reason it was obvious the door at the top was closed. Opening that door and walking into the kitchen seemed foolhardy at best. If he was shot, Kinsey and Frances would be sitting ducks.

He stood there for a second, trying to orient himself. The washroom was at the back of the house, but this part of the basement was right under the living area. He needed to be quieter now than he'd been before. He felt his way carefully to the outside wall and reached up to feel the rough texture of old wood. Sure enough, someone had nailed boards over the glass.

After numerous attempts and failures, he finally found one board that wasn't nailed in as well as the others. He pushed a nearby box beneath the window to improve leverage and managed to pull and twist it free. That provided adequate light to see that there were four windows in a row, all boarded up. Each was about eighteen inches high and a couple of feet long. He needed to find a tool to help himself and fumbled around for several moments until an old golf club caught his attention.

And that's when he heard a tapping noise coming from the window he'd partially uncovered. The noise came again and he realized it originated outside. He had no idea who or what he'd find, but as he didn't have a whole lot to lose, he used the gold club to pop off another board.

A man had crouched down to be able to see through the window. Zane couldn't believe it when the heavily shadowed figure materialized into Detective Woods. Woods pantomimed his reluctance to talk, pointing overhead. Zane realized they were directly under the kitchen.

And yet, this was something of a miracle and what was the saying, fortune favors the bold? Using the head of the golf club, he tapped on the glass until it shattered, wincing at the noise it made. The windows were from before the age of safety glass and jagged pieces gleamed like vampire fangs. He took off his jacket and tried to brush some of them away as Woods leaned in close.

"I came looking for you when you didn't show up at the impound yard or my office," he said. "After the last week or so, I figured almost anything could have happened."

"James Fenwick and the man Kinsey knew as Ryan Jones are upstairs and they're armed.

They're behind everything. They're waiting until dark to get rid of us. We have to get out of here."

"I knocked on the door first," Woods said. "No one answered, but I knew they were in there and that got me curious. When I saw your rental parked down the block, I decided to do a little snooping. These boarded-up windows looked suspicious. Where are the others? Anyone hurt?"

"They're close by. I'll get them."

"Hurry. I'll call for backup and work on this glass."

Zane rushed back to the washroom. He found Kinsey and her grandmother standing apart, not looking at each other. "Come on," he urged. "We have a way out."

They didn't need coaxing. The three of them arrived back at the window to find that Woods had draped his suit coat over the sill. Zane helped Frances climb on top of the box. With Zane shoving from behind while Woods pulled from outside, Frances twisted her body sideways to fit through the jagged opening. She was almost out when a startled scream jumped from her throat. She swallowed it back almost immediately. "I'm sorry, I'm sorry, I cut my leg."

"We'll take care of it in a minute," Woods said. "Stay low and quiet." He turned back to Zane. "Let me work on this piece of glass before Kinsey and you come through."

"Hurry," Zane urged as Kinsey stepped onto

the box. He caught her hand and pressed it against his lips. "I love you," he said.

As she looked down at him, a smile spread her beautiful ruby lips. "I love you, too."

"I think I got it," Woods said. "Give it a try."

As she began to hoist herself up, Zane heard a noise coming from the top of the stairs. The door was still closed, but the light came on. Zane ran for the stairs, climbing two at a time, rushing as fast as he could. If either man entered the stairwell, they'd catch Kinsey in the act of leaving. He had to stop them.

James appeared right as Zane burst into the kitchen. Zane slugged him square on the jaw and caught his shoulders as he slumped. The other door opened. Ryan paused midstep, but he recovered quickly and the semiautomatic he'd flaunted in the basement appeared in his hand. Zane did the only thing he could think to do to keep from taking a bullet in the gut. He shoved James Fenwick at Ryan with every ounce of strength he still possessed.

The gun went off before both men hit the floor. Zane was already in motion, following them. When he caught a glimpse of the gun in Ryan's hand, he kicked as hard as he could. The gun spun across the room.

Zane scrambled to retrieve it and held it on Ryan as Ryan shoved James's limp body off of his. They stared at each other while a pounding on the stairs preceded Detective Woods's abrupt arrival in the kitchen, weapon drawn. "You're bleeding," he said after a quick survey.

Zane glanced down at his side. His white shirt was stained red where the bullet that had killed James Fenwick had apparently passed through his body and nicked Zane's rib cage. "Just a graze."

"Please, sit down before you fall down. I've got him."

Zane shook his head. "Not until I see Kinsey."

"She'll be out front by now."

Zane stepped around James Fenwick's body without a second glance. He opened the front door and saw Kinsey and Frances standing next to a squad car. Kinsey turned. For the first time in over two years he felt whole and complete again.

And the reason was running toward him.

"I'M NERVOUS," KINSEY ADMITTED as Zane turned onto ranch land. He stopped his truck in front of his father's house. To the world, legally, they were Sandra and Gerard, but to each other, the old names were the ones they used.

"I don't blame you, sweetheart," he said, "but I think you'll like Grace when you get to know her."

Even as he spoke, the side door opened and a delicate-looking woman with graying brown hair appeared. Kinsey didn't need anyone to tell her that she was looking at her mother, who rushed out onto the porch and then stopped. She clasped her hands together and held them against her chest as though struggling to keep her heart from leaping from her body.

Kinsey got out of the truck and walked up the stairs. She wasn't sure what to say or how to act. Even thinking of anyone other than Frances as her mother felt wrong somehow.

Grace reached out and took Kinsey's hands. "Sandra," she said softly. "Oh, my dear, I can hardly believe it's you."

They sat down on the narrow bench, searching each other's faces. Finally Grace cleared her throat. "How is my mother holding up? I know it's been two weeks since, well, everything happened. I wanted to come to New Orleans, but I wasn't sure it was the right thing to do..."

"Please," Kinsey said softly. "It's okay. It's been a really busy two weeks. Anyway, Frances is being extradited back to Idaho. I'm not sure what charges they'll bring against her. It's hard for me to believe she actually murdered my father."

Grace's grip on Kinsey's hands tightened. "About that...you need to understand something. I was different back then. Selfish and stupid...into drugs...my marriage was a joke. Greg was...difficult and high all the time. He kept making me ask my mother for money and she always came through, except for the last time, when she refused. She said we needed to grow up and take care of our baby, get sober... of course, she was right."

They were talking about Frances, or technically, Mary. Kinsey had to constantly remind herself about the truth of the relationships she'd taken for granted her entire life. The falsehoods and lies still roamed her mind and heart like a pride of caged lions.

"That last day I was passed out in the bedroom," Grace continued. "Greg and you were in the living room. The police said he'd just finished cleaning his gun. All the supplies were still on the table. And he was high as usual. Mom came to the house to pick you up and take you back to her place. She took care of you a lot, almost all the time. Anyway, Greg was furious with her for not giving us the money we'd asked for. They got into an argument... I know because their yelling woke me up. You wouldn't stop crying. It was terrible.

"I tried to get up to help, but I couldn't get my balance...I was too wasted. I heard Greg tell my mother to leave. She pleaded with him to let her take you with her, that you were crying and needed a clean diaper. He said she would never see you again, period. Again I tried to get control of myself, but I couldn't focus. Your cries became screams. I guess Greg took out his aggression on the most innocent person in the room. My mother shouted for Greg to stop hitting you. She begged him. And then there was a gunshot…it got real quiet."

"You don't have to finish this," Kinsey said in a shaky voice.

Grace swallowed hard. "Yes, I do. Eventually I made it out to the living room. Greg lay on the floor, his revolver next to him. The door was wide open. You and my mother were gone."

Kinsey wiped tears off her cheeks. Zane was suddenly standing beside her. He handed her a clean folded handkerchief. A sense of peace flooded her body as he gently smoothed her hair.

"I'm sorry to have to tell you all this," Grace whispered. "I'm sorry you have to know what your father and I were like. I didn't protect you. My mother did in the only way she thought she could. I want you to know that I've spoken with the district attorney and begged him to consider all the facts before he brings her to trial. But if it comes to that, I'll speak out for her."

"Thank you for being so honest," Kinsey mumbled, and then she spontaneously hugged her mother. "I know it can't be easy for you," she added.

Her mother straightened up but kept her hands around Kinsey's. "I don't expect you to forgive me or your grandmother for what we've done to your life, but please know it wasn't intentional. Until two weeks ago, I thought both of you were dead. When I got that letter and Gerard agreed to go see what he could find out, I never dreamed I was sending him into such danger. I just had to know. I've lived my life in shame and guilt."

"I think you both have," Kinsey said. "Maybe it's time to stop."

Grace hugged Kinsey this time and that caused a new flood of tears. Finally she spoke again. "I've talked to your father, Gerard, and he promises me we'll help my mother financially. How do we go about getting decent legal help?"

"It's taken care of," Zane said. "The lawyer who drew up Bill's will made sure the inheritance came to her. His practice will defend her if it comes to trial. As for finances, there was a room built behind library shelves crammed with art and old books, antiques, even a crusty old trunk of gold doubloons—Bill was quite a collector. She'll be okay."

"And the man who almost killed you?"

"Which time?" Zane asked with a fleeting smile. "The lawyer pushed me into the street and tried to choke me in the hospital, Ryan threw a toolbox on top of us and forced us into the slough."

"I was thinking about the shooting."

"Ah, Ryan. Aka, Chad Dodge, Kevin Lester and

a bunch of other names. The police have enough on him to keep him behind bars for decades."

Someone inside the house yelled Grace's name and Kinsey stood. "Is that Lily?" she asked. "I've been worried about her."

Chance showed up in the open door. "Don't you know?" he asked. "Lily is gone. She left the same day you and Gerard did."

"Where did she go?" Kinsey asked.

Chance shook his head. "Just took off. Her and Charlie both. I don't know where they went. Frankly, I don't care."

They all looked at each other for a long moment, Chance's last declaration hanging in the air like acrid smoke. And then Zane put his arm around his brother's shoulder and Chance's bravado slipped off his face.

Kinsey closed her eyes for a moment, unable to bear any more emotion. She heard retreating footsteps as everyone apparently went inside the house, but a second later, familiar hands clasped hers and pulled her against his chest. She opened her eyes and looked up at Zane.

"Let's go home," he said as he leaned down to kiss her.

"That sounds wonderful," she whispered against his lips.

Home. At last.

* * * * *

Alice Sharpe's miniseries,
THE BROTHERS OF
HASTINGS RIDGE RANCH,
continues later this year.
Look for it
wherever Harlequin Intrigue books
and ebooks are sold!

LARGER-PRINT BOOKS!

HARLEQUIN

Presents®

GET 2 FREE LARGER-PRINT NOVELS PLUS 2 FREE GIFTS!

PASSION
GUARANTEED
SEDUCTION

YES! Please send me 2 FREE LARGER-PRINT Harlequin Presents® novels and my 2 FREE gifts (gifts are worth about $10). After receiving them, if I don't wish to receive any more books, I can return the shipping statement marked "cancel." If I don't cancel, I will receive 6 brand-new novels every month and be billed just $5.30 per book in the U.S. or $5.74 per book in Canada. That's a saving of at least 12% off the cover price! It's quite a bargain! Shipping and handling is just 50¢ per book in the U.S. and 75¢ per book in Canada.* I understand that accepting the 2 free books and gifts places me under no obligation to buy anything. I can always return a shipment and cancel at any time. Even if I never buy another book, the two free books and gifts are mine to keep forever.

176/376 HDN GHVY

Name	(PLEASE PRINT)	
Address		Apt. #
City	State/Prov.	Zip/Postal Code

Signature (if under 18, a parent or guardian must sign)

LARGER-PRINT BOOKS!
GET 2 FREE LARGER-PRINT NOVELS PLUS
2 FREE GIFTS!

H HARLEQUIN®

Romance

From the Heart, For the Heart

YES! Please send me 2 FREE LARGER-PRINT Harlequin® Romance novels and my 2 FREE gifts (gifts are worth about $10). After receiving them, if I don't wish to receive any more books, I can return the shipping statement marked "cancel." If I don't cancel, I will receive 4 brand-new novels every month and be billed just $5.09 per book in the U.S. or $5.49 per book in Canada. That's a savings of at least 15% off the cover price! It's quite a bargain! Shipping and handling is just 50¢ per book in the U.S. and 75¢ per book in Canada.* I understand that accepting the 2 free books and gifts places me under no obligation to buy anything. I can always return a shipment and cancel at any time. Even if I never buy another book, the two free books and gifts are mine to keep forever.

119/319 HDN GHWC

Name	(PLEASE PRINT)	

Address		Apt. #

City	State/Prov.	Zip/Postal Code

Signature (if under 18, a parent or guardian must sign)

Mail to the Reader Service:
IN U.S.A.: P.O. Box 1867, Buffalo, NY 14240-1867
IN CANADA: P.O. Box 609, Fort Erie, Ontario L2A 5X3

Want to try two free books from another line?
Call 1-800-873-8635 or visit www.ReaderService.com.

* Terms and prices subject to change without notice. Prices do not include applicable taxes. Sales tax applicable in N.Y. Canadian residents will be charged applicable taxes. Offer not valid in Quebec. This offer is limited to one order per household. Not valid for current subscribers to Harlequin Romance Larger-Print books. All orders subject to credit approval. Credit or debit balances in a customer's account(s) may be offset by any other outstanding balance owed by or to the customer. Please allow 4 to 6 weeks for delivery. Offer available while quantities last.

Your Privacy—The Reader Service is committed to protecting your privacy. Our Privacy Policy is available online at www.ReaderService.com or upon request from the Reader Service.

We make a portion of our mailing list available to reputable third parties that offer products we believe may interest you. If you prefer that we not exchange your name with third parties, or if you wish to clarify or modify your communication preferences, please visit us at www.ReaderService.com/consumerchoice or write to us at Reader Service Preference Service, P.O. Box 9062, Buffalo, NY 14240-9062. Include your complete name and address.

HRLP15